W9-CHN-834

"Until we get some answers about this case, I'm your bodyguard," John said

"Oh, no, you're not," Andrea protested.

"Do you have any other ideas?"

"Yes. You find out who killed Wingate and I leave."

"Try again."

"I'll go someplace safe and give you a number where I can be reached."

He shook his head. "You're my key witness. I'm not letting you out of my sight."

She glanced at the door. Maybe she should run for it. Maybe it was her only chance to get out of this mess.

Ridiculous.

But equally ridiculous was the idea of John as her bodyguard. No, not ridiculous. Dangerous. Because even now, with his questions and threats still ringing in her ears, she could hear the loneliness in his voice.

And she could feel her heart respond.

Dear Harlequin Intrigue Reader,

This month Harlequin Intrigue has an enthralling array of breathtaking romantic suspense to make the most of those last lingering days of summer.

The wait is finally over! The next crop of undercover agents who belong to the newest branch of the top secret Confidential organization are about to embark on an unbelievable adventure. Award-winning reader favorite Gayle Wilson will rivet you with the launch book of this brand-new ten-story continuity series. COLORADO CONFIDENTIAL will begin in Harlequin Intrigue, break out into a special release anthology and finish in Harlequin Historicals. In *Rocky Mountain Maverick*, an undeniably sexy undercover agent infiltrates a powerful senator's ranch and falls under the influence of an intoxicating impostor. Be there from the very beginning!

The adrenaline rush continues in *The Butler's Daughter* by Joyce Sullivan, with the first book in her new miniseries, THE COLLINGWOOD HEIRS. A beautiful guardian has been entrusted with the care of a toddler-sized heir, but now they are running for their lives and she must place their safety in an enigmatic protector's tantalizing hands! Ann Voss Peterson heats things up with *Incriminating Passion* when a targeted "witness" to a murder manages to inflame the heart of a by-the-book assistant D.A.

Finally rounding out the month is *Semiautomatic Marriage* by veteran author Leona Karr. Will the race to track down a killer culminate in a *real* trip down the aisle for an undercover husband and wife?

So pick up all four of these pulse-pounding stories and end the summer with a bang!

Sincerely,

Denise O'Sullivan
Harlequin Intrigue, Senior Editor

INCRIMINATING PASSION

ANN VOSS PETERSON

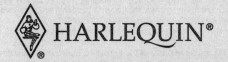

HARLEQUIN®

TORONTO • NEW YORK • LONDON
AMSTERDAM • PARIS • SYDNEY • HAMBURG
STOCKHOLM • ATHENS • TOKYO • MILAN • MADRID
PRAGUE • WARSAW • BUDAPEST • AUCKLAND

If you purchased this book without a cover you should be aware that this book is stolen property. It was reported as "unsold and destroyed" to the publisher, and neither the author nor the publisher has received any payment for this "stripped book."

ISBN 0-373-22723-X

INCRIMINATING PASSION

Copyright © 2003 by Ann Voss Peterson

All rights reserved. Except for use in any review, the reproduction or utilization of this work in whole or in part in any form by any electronic, mechanical or other means, now known or hereafter invented, including xerography, photocopying and recording, or in any information storage or retrieval system, is forbidden without the written permission of the publisher, Harlequin Enterprises Limited, 225 Duncan Mill Road, Don Mills, Ontario, Canada M3B 3K9.

All characters in this book have no existence outside the imagination of the author and have no relation whatsoever to anyone bearing the same name or names. They are not even distantly inspired by any individual known or unknown to the author, and all incidents are pure invention.

This edition published by arrangement with Harlequin Books S.A.

® and TM are trademarks of the publisher. Trademarks indicated with ® are registered in the United States Patent and Trademark Office, the Canadian Trade Marks Office and in other countries.

Visit us at www.eHarlequin.com

Printed in U.S.A.

ABOUT THE AUTHOR

Ever since she was a little girl making her own books out of construction paper, Ann Voss Peterson wanted to write. So when it came time to choose a major at the University of Wisconsin, creative writing was her only choice. Of course, writing wasn't a *practical* choice—one needs to earn a living. So Ann found jobs ranging from proofreading legal transcripts to working with quarter horses to washing windows. But no matter how she earned her paycheck, she continued to write the type of stories that captured her heart and imagination—romantic suspense. Ann lives near Madison, Wisconsin, with her husband, her two young sons, her Border collie and her quarter horse mare. Ann loves to hear from readers. E-mail her at ann@annvosspeterson.com or visit her Web site at annvosspeterson.com.

Books by Ann Voss Peterson

HARLEQUIN INTRIGUE

579—INADMISSIBLE PASSION
618—HIS WITNESS, HER CHILD
647—ACCESSORY TO MARRIAGE
674—LAYING DOWN THE LAW
684—GYPSY MAGIC
     "Sabina"
702—CLAIMING HIS FAMILY
723—INCRIMINATING PASSION

Don't miss any of our special offers. Write to us at the following address for information on our newest releases.

Harlequin Reader Service
U.S.: 3010 Walden Ave., P.O. Box 1325, Buffalo, NY 14269
Canadian: P.O. Box 609, Fort Erie, Ont. L2A 5X3

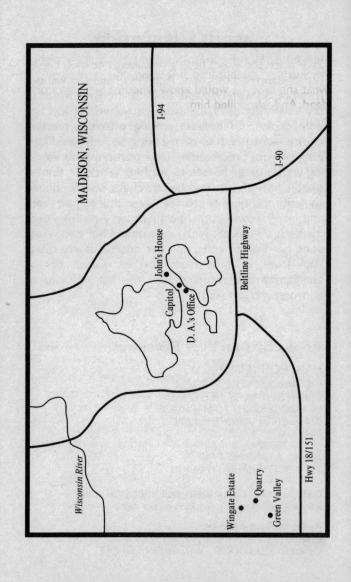

MADISON, WISCONSIN

I-94

I-90

John's House

Capitol

D. A.'s Office

Beltline Highway

Wisconsin River

Wingate Estate

Quarry

Green Valley

Hwy 18/151

CAST OF CHARACTERS

Andrea Kirkland—She witnessed *something* the night her husband disappeared. If she can only remember what she saw, she would know whether he is alive or dead. And who killed him.

John Cohen—A burned-out, cynical assistant district attorney, John doesn't believe in anything or anybody. That is, not until a desperate, tattered Andrea walks into his office and challenges his heart.

Wingate Kirkland—The powerful, abusive multimillionaire is missing—or dead.

Joyce Pratt—Wingate Kirkland's sister, Joyce blames Andrea for her brother's disappearance.

Melvin Pratt—Joyce's husband's favorite words are *yes* and *dear*. Is this meek man hiding a dangerous side?

Gary Putnam—The small-town police chief has Andrea in his sights.

Tonnie Bartell—Was the brunette bombshell trying to take Andrea's place?

Ruthie Banks—Andrea's neighbor says she witnessed something fishy going on at the estate. Is she telling the truth?

Judge Gerald Banks—Known as the hanging judge, Gerald Banks is out to see that Andrea is locked away for good.

Hank Sutcliffe—The beefy blond Adonis is hiding something. The question is, will that something clear Andrea or put her behind bars?

Marcella Hernandez—How far will the housekeeper go to protect what she loves?

To John.
Thanks for the love, the support
and the inspiration.

Chapter One

Andrea Kirkland clutched the steering wheel with trembling hands and squinted into the rearview mirror. The black pickup pulled closer. So close the headlights glared through the back window of her Lexus.

Flipping the mirror to cut the reflection, she forced herself to draw in a deep breath. The truck's driver was probably just in a hurry. He couldn't have anything to do with the memories she had suppressed, the memories that had finally broken through this evening. Memories of her husband Wingate crumpling to the floor, of his blood soaking into the Persian rug, of his fixed stare.

She eased her car close to the edge of the country highway to allow the truck to pass. She was going as fast as she dared on the dark road. If he was in such a hurry, he would have to go around.

The truck remained glued to her bumper.

Andrea's throat closed. Fear scrambled up her

spine. The road was straight for another quarter mile. Then it grew curvy as it wound its way around the quarry. Any ordinary impatient driver would have grabbed the opportunity to pass while he still could.

Unless this was no ordinary impatient driver.

Her heart slammed against her ribs. She hadn't told anyone her memories were returning. Not when they'd started filtering back in flashes of nightmares, nor when she'd put all the pieces together this evening, after the crack of deer hunters' rifles had her break out in a cold sweat.

She'd made a single call. To the tiny Green Valley police station. And explained her memories to a single person—the receptionist. But when Ruthie had told her all three officers in the department were busy on a call, she'd decided she couldn't wait. She had to get away from that house. Away from the memories of blood. Of death. So she'd set out for the police station.

And now here she was with a black truck breathing down her neck.

She didn't need the rearview mirror to know the truck's bumper was only inches from hers. She swallowed the fear rising in her throat and piloted the Lexus into a sweeping curve. Trees lined the edge of the road. The sparkle of moonlight on water glittered through thinning autumn leaves. The police station was still a good three miles away. On the other side of the old quarry. On the other side of the world.

Her hands were damp, slippery on the steering wheel's leather cover. Another sharper curve loomed ahead. She pushed her foot down on the accelerator. Surely her sporty Lexus could take a turn better than the large, boxy truck behind her. She swept into the turn just as she felt the first hit on her bumper.

The steering wheel jumped in her hands. She tightened her grip, digging her nails into the leather. Pulling her foot from the accelerator, she fought to gain control.

The truck swerved into the opposite lane and pulled up beside her. Its windows stared down at her, tinted black. Its shadow loomed beside her like a specter of death.

Oh God.

The truck's side slammed against the Lexus. Steel screeched against steel. Her neck snapped to the side. The wheel ripped from her grip. She fought to regain control, fingers slipping on leather.

The truck drew back and hit again, plowing its side into her. Pushing her off the road. Toward the steep bank. Toward the moonlit water of the old quarry.

No.

Tires skidded on pavement, on gravel. She gripped the wheel with all her strength, trying to right the car, trying to keep from plunging down the bank and into the water.

The truck hit again, its full weight slamming into her car. Steel buckled. Wheels churned, spewing gravel. Scrub brush and tree branches scraped against her car like frantic fingers. But nothing could slow her down. Nothing could stop her.

Andrea braced herself and prayed. The Lexus flew over the edge, weightless for a moment. Then gravity dragged her down to the black water below.

She hit the surface with a bone-jarring thud. Her head lurched forward like a rag doll's. Her forehead grazed the steering wheel, her body held in the seat only by her seat belt. The car dipped low and sprang backward. It bucked on the waves before settling in the black water.

Andrea's head rang with the impact. Dizziness threatened to swamp her, to pull her under.

Black water swirled around the car and lapped over the hood. The headlights glowed, already under the water, the heavy engine dragging her down. Frigid water crept over the pedals and up the floorboards, lapping at her feet.

Oh God, she was going to sink like a stone.

She had to clear her mind. She had to get out of this car before it was too late.

She lurched forward, trying to move, but something pinned her to the seat. The seat belt. She had to release the seat belt. Concentrating hard, she made her unsteady fingers close over the latch and push the release button. Nothing. The belt still held. She pushed the button again. It still didn't release. Forcing herself to hold on to some shred of calm, she jammed the button as hard as she could. The belt pulled free.

Pain throbbed in her head and shot down her neck with each movement. Nausea swirled in her stomach. Black water washed against the door and the front corner of the window. She had to get out. Now. She pressed the button to lower the power window. Nothing. Heart in her throat, she tried all the buttons. No luck. The water had short-circuited the windows. She would have to open the door and hope she could get out of the car before the black water swamped it.

She groped a hand along the door. Her fingers brushed the cool steel handle. She'd have one chance. Once she opened the door, the water would rush into the car. It would fill in a matter of seconds. She had only one chance to get clear of the sinking hulk of steel before she was dragged to the bottom.

Drawing in a deep breath of courage, she grasped the door handle and pulled. The latch released. She pushed the door with her shoulder.

It didn't move.

She shoved again with all her strength.

It wouldn't open. Water pressed against the door, keeping it shut as effectively as if whoever had run her off the road was on the other side, pushing it closed. Waiting for her to drown.

She closed her eyes, struggling to keep a lid on her panic. She had to think. There had to be a way out.

A chill of fear claimed her, causing her whole body to convulse. She would have to let the car sink. She would have to let it fill with water until the pressure outside the car and inside the car equalized. Then she could push the door open and swim to the surface.

She would have to wait.

She had no idea how deep the quarry was, or how steep the walls. The car might flip on the way down, rolling down the sheer wall until she was so disoriented or injured that she couldn't escape. But there was no other way out. The doors were sealed. The windows inoperable. She would have to take her chances.

The car listed forward, dragged downward by the engine. The water rose. To her knees. To her waist. To her shoulders. She lifted her head so she could breath the shrinking pocket of air. The water kept rising.

Finally, with one last belch, the car nosed forward and plunged for the bottom.

Head near the ceiling, she could still breath from a pocket of trapped air. She could last until the car hit bottom.

Unless it flipped.

The front bumper jarred against stone. Andrea pitched forward. She gulped in a last breath of air. Water closed over her head. Her chin came down hard on the steering wheel. Her teeth clamped together, catching the inside of her cheek. The copper taste of blood flooded her mouth. For a moment, she seemed suspended. The car swayed.

And flipped.

The roof hit rock. Andrea twisted, her body flopped forward, her back landing hard on the car's ceiling. The car stopped, resting upside down on the quarry floor.

Andrea groped for the door. Her fingers closed around the handle. She pulled the lever and shoved the door open. One strong thrust with her legs and she was out of the car. She kicked and thrashed, battling for the surface.

The water was cold, so cold. Her lungs burned for air. She kicked harder. Faster. Her pulse thundered in her ears. Her lungs felt as if they would explode. Her clothing dragged at her, pulling her down, her shoes making each kick clumsy.

Finally, her head broke the surface. She gasped for breath, pulling air into burning lungs. Scissoring her legs, she trod water, gulping breath after breath.

Once she felt strong enough, she swam to shore and crawled out on the steep bank. Rocks dug into her hands and knees. Her body shivered uncontrollably. But she had made it. She was alive.

Now she had to make sure she stayed that way.

Chapter Two

Assistant District Attorney John Cohen trudged out of the courtroom and down the hall to the elevator on the way back to his office. Thank God the day was almost over. He'd won another case, put another scumbag in a long line of scumbags behind bars for a few more months, and added to his impressive conviction record. He should be happy. He should be looking forward to a night out with friends, to lifting a glass in celebration. But the only thing he wanted to do was go home, collapse into his recliner and forget the whole depressing mess his life had become.

When he'd taken the job with the district attorney's office, he'd had aspirations of justice and making the world a better place. But after fifteen years of prosecuting the scum of the earth, only to have viler scum replace them while they did their too-short stints in prison, it was getting harder to drag himself to work each day. He felt more and more as if he was fighting a losing battle. As if his soul was being weighed down with the evil of life.

He needed a vacation. A vacation that would last the rest of his years.

The elevator door slid open. It was almost full. Just his luck. He crowded inside and hit the button for the fifth floor, trying not to breathe the air, sour with tension and stale sweat.

"Hold the door, please."

Reflexively he reached out his arm to stop the door from sliding shut.

A slip of a woman with stringy blond hair and bruises marring her forehead and chin darted into the elevator. Her eyes met John's for an instant, their depths pale blue and glassy, as if she'd gotten too little sleep or done too many drugs or just plain seen too much of the sordid underbelly of life. She turned her back to him and focused on the lighted numbers over the door.

John resisted the hypnotic tradition of staring at the numbers. Instead, he stared at the top of the new-comer's head and tried to guess whether she was a battered woman coming to plead for her husband's release so he could go home and punish her for call-ing the cops in the first place, or a prostitute strug-gling to look reformed for a court date. Her petite body and slender curves evident even under the jacket pulled tight around her shoulders made him think she had the goods to be a prostitute. And a successful one at that. But the bruises, her lack of makeup, and the silent desperation in her eyes settled it. She was here to plead for her husband.

He shook his head. Not that it made much of a difference. She was stuck in a hell of a life either way. A hell of a life that he sure couldn't rescue her from. God knew he'd tried before with other women. And he'd failed miserably each and every time.

He directed his gaze to the numbers over the door, determined not to think about the woman in front of him too hard. Just the idea of a man laying a hand on that slender neck made his blood boil. Or at least simmer. His blood was too thick to reach boiling anymore. These days it only hardened and burned.

When the door opened he followed her down the hall and into the district attorney's office. There he left her waiting to speak with a receptionist while he walked to his glorified cubicle and dropped his briefcase on a chair. He had nothing left to do but hop a bus and return to his empty two-flat dump. To his recliner, a dinner of cold pizza and a good stiff drink. In fact, since his big, empty house was within stumbling distance of the office, a good stiff drink was in order right now. He was just reaching for the bottle of Jack Daniels in the bottom drawer of his desk when his phone rang.

He held the receiver to his ear. "Yeah."

"Mr. Cohen?" The new receptionist's voice melted over the line like warm honey.

Chantel was her name, if he remembered correctly. A welcome change from Maggie. He pushed the thought of the former receptionist from his mind. He didn't like to think about her. How she'd tried to set him up to take the fall for fixing a case that set serial rapist Andrew Clarke Smythe free. How she'd almost succeeded. And, worst of all, how she'd utterly ruined his taste for ketchup. "Do you know what time it is, Chantel?"

"I know. And I'm sorry. I know you just returned from court."

He heaved a breath and released it into the phone. "It's all right. What do you have for me?"

"I have a woman here who needs to talk to someone."

There'd been only one woman in the reception area when he'd entered the office. The one he'd seen in the elevator. He exhaled a stream of air through tight lips. He was tired. Exhausted. He'd had it with sad, dead-end stories. The last thing he wanted was to get involved in another. He should tell the receptionist to find another assistant district attorney to talk to the woman or tell her to come back tomorrow. But something wouldn't let him push the words past his lips.

Maybe it was the desperation he'd seen in her pale-blue eyes. Maybe it was the fear plain on her face. Hell, maybe it was simply the urge to be near that saucy little body again. He grimaced. He was even more cynical than he'd given himself credit for. "Send her in."

He had replaced the receiver and relocked the booze drawer when a timid knock sounded on his door. "Come in."

She pushed the door open and stepped inside before recognition registered on her face. "I saw you on the elevator."

"You sure did." He half rose from his chair and held out a hand. "The name's John Cohen."

She reached out and shook his hand. Her skin was soft, her nails perfectly manicured. Quite a contrast to her stringy hair and desperate look.

"And what brings you here today?"

"I need your help. I don't know where else to turn." She met his gaze with an urgency that made his gut tighten.

He pushed the unease aside. He couldn't afford to feel for this woman, no matter how desperate she seemed. Once he let himself feel, expectations were right around the corner. And once he started to expect too much, disappointment was inevitable. It was a mistake he'd made many times before. And it was one he damn well wasn't going to repeat.

"Why don't you have a seat and tell me about it?" The words automatically tripped off his tongue. Maybe he should be a shrink. He could psychoanalyze himself during off hours. Save a bundle of money.

She lowered herself into one of the chairs in front of his desk.

He sank into his own chair. Gluing his gaze to hers, he waited for her to begin.

"It's about my husband."

Damn. Could he call them or what? A leaden weight settled in his gut. He'd been doing this job far too long. He braced himself for the rest of her sad story—a story he likely couldn't do a damn thing to make end happily. "What about your husband? Is he a ward of the county?"

"What?"

"Is he in jail?"

"Not hardly." She frowned and drew a slow breath as if to steel herself. "I'm Andrea Kirkland. Wingate Kirkland's wife."

John sat forward in his chair. He'd thought he'd run out of surprises during the past few years, but this certainly qualified as a change of pace. "Wingate Kirkland?"

She pursed her lips together and nodded.

Even though John didn't exactly rub shoulders with the movers and shakers in Dane County, he'd sure as hell heard of Wingate Kirkland. Everyone had heard of Wingate Kirkland. The millionaire and his money were single-handedly responsible for reclaiming countless landmarks in Madison's historic downtown. Of course, once reclaimed, he turned them into condos and rented them to anyone who could pay. Capitalism in action.

He narrowed his eyes on the woman in front of him. The manicured nails and doe-soft skin fit the image he had of Kirkland's wife. But the stringy hair, the bruises and the desperate glint in her eyes were another story. "And what is it you want to tell me about your husband?"

"He's dead. Murdered. And whoever killed him is after me."

Second shocker in a row. John blew a breath through pursed lips, creating a soft whistle. Wingate Kirkland. Murdered. So even living in a gated rural estate and having more money than God couldn't isolate a person from violence and villainy. What else was new? "Why haven't I heard about this? I would think the news media would be all over Wingate Kirkland's death."

She gripped the arms of her chair. "No one knows yet."

He raised his brows. "Why don't you start from the beginning?"

"I don't know what the beginning is exactly."

"Then start as close as you can. When was your husband killed?"

"About a week ago, I think."

"A week ago? You *think?*" He didn't even try to keep the incredulity out of his voice. The rich really were a different breed from the rest of the human race. "Glad you could take time out from your busy schedule to finally report it."

She raised her chin and looked him square in the eye. A show of superiority. An empty show, if her nervous fingers tangling together in her lap were any indication. "I would have reported it, but…"

"But what?"

"But I didn't remember it until last night."

"Your husband's murder just slipped your mind?"

She untwined her fingers and splayed her hands in front of her in a pleading pose. "I must have blocked it. I mean, that happens sometimes, doesn't it? My mind must have blocked out the murder until I was better able to deal with it."

Maybe he should have had that belt of Jack before agreeing to talk to this woman. He needed a good buzz in order to swallow this wild tale. "Are you suggesting you had amnesia?"

"I guess. I don't know. All I know is that except for some nightmares, I thought my life was business-as-usual up until last night."

"Except you had no husband. I take it a body hasn't been found."

She shook her head.

"Do you know who killed him?"

"No."

"This sounds more like a missing person's case than a murder. Have you filled out a report with the police?"

"No."

"When did you realize he was gone?"

"Just last night. When the memories—"

"When you remembered your husband had been missing for a week."

She raised her chin at the suspicion in his tone. "I thought he was away on business. His real-estate development company is based in Chicago. He's down there most of the time."

Incredible. The woman seemed to have an answer to everything. "Was he often gone for a week at a time without giving you so much as a phone call?"

"We didn't have the greatest marriage, Mr. Cohen. In fact, we didn't have much of a marriage at all. He kept me around for show on the rare occasions he needed a trophy wife. And he said he wanted an heir eventually. Otherwise, Win didn't have a lot of use for me."

"So why did you marry him?"

"I had my reasons."

"I'll bet you had a few million of them."

Her lips pursed and her eyes narrowed to blue bands. "I didn't marry him for his money, if that's what you're implying. Not really."

"Then why did you *really* marry him?"

"Listen, I didn't want to come here. I can take care of myself. I don't want yours or anyone else's help. But a man is dead, and I thought you might care to know about *that*."

"But you say you can't tell me much about that, Mrs. Kirkland. So I need to know all you *can* tell me about your husband. Including what his marriage was like."

She pushed a defeated breath through tight lips. "Fine. My father left when I was young. Win was a father figure, I guess. He took care of me, offered me security. I was eighteen when I married him. It's not something I'm proud of."

"Then why did you stay married to him?"

"Win made it clear he didn't want me to leave."

"He threatened you?"

"Yes."

"With violence?"

"At times."

John's gut tightened. So he'd called Andrea Kirkland right after all.

She raised her chin again, a flash of fire smoldering in the depths of her eyes. "I was leaving him anyway. I had made arrangements, set aside money. I was leaving that night—the night I saw him murdered."

Time for John's eyes to widen again. "You *witnessed* the murder?"

"Yes. But I don't remember much about it. Just the gunshots. And Win's head resting on the Persian rug. And all the blood...." She dropped her gaze to his desk and studied the wood grain for a full minute. Crossing her arms, she rubbed her hands over them as if she was cold. She looked like that little girl in search of a father figure she'd talked about. Desperate, vulnerable, yet determined to go it on her own.

An ache settled in John's shoulders. He shouldn't care about her vulnerability. He shouldn't care that her husband had used threats of violence to keep her in line. He shouldn't care at all about her bizarre tale. He should merely do his job and go home to that recliner and stiff drink. "Have you told the police you witnessed a murder?"

She swallowed hard and met his gaze. "I tried."

"But?"

"I called the Green Valley police station last night, but all the officers were out on a call. I told Ruthie, the woman who answers the phone, the things I remembered and that I was driving in. I didn't want to stay in that house one more second." She paused as if hesitant to go on.

"And?"

"On my way a black pickup truck ran me off the road. My car is at the bottom of the Green Valley quarry."

He crooked a brow. "That old quarry is full of water."

"Good thing. Otherwise I would have crashed and died. As it was, I only had to worry about drowning."

Yet another surprise. That old quarry was deep as hell itself. And this time of year it would be bone-cold as well. Somehow this petite woman had managed to free herself from certain death. She must be a lot stronger—and even more determined—than she looked.

He took hold of the stirrings of admiration. He couldn't go there, couldn't start weaving her into some sort of heroine in his mind. Or some sort of victim in need of his protection. Not unless he wanted to give reality an opening to bite him in the ass like a snarling dog. He reached for the phone. "I'll call the Green Valley police right now. They can investigate your claims and we'll see what we can do."

Her eyes sprang wide. She lunged for his hand. Her fingers clamped down hard, preventing him from lifting the phone out of its cradle. "No police. Please."

"That's how cases like this are handled, Mrs. Kirkland. The police investigate the crime. I prosecute the offender."

Her gaze landed on her hand gripping his. She yanked her hand back as if afraid he would bite. But she didn't sit back in her chair. She stood at the edge of his desk, every muscle in her body rigid. "You can't call the Green Valley police."

He pulled his hand from the phone, leaving the receiver in the cradle. "You'd better give me a good reason."

"The police were the only ones who knew I remembered what happened to Win. I called the station, then suddenly this truck showed up and tried to kill me.''

''And you think someone in the police department was in that truck?''

''Wouldn't you?''

She had him there. But where did that leave him? If he couldn't call the police and have them check out her story, what was he going to do with this woman?

He glanced at his watch. Almost six o'clock. Except for a few assistant district attorneys preparing for court tomorrow morning, the office would be empty. That ruled out foisting this woman off on a junior ADA. ''Do you have any family you can stay with until we can figure out what's going on here?''

''Win has a sister, but we aren't exactly close.''

''How about friends?''

She shook her head.

The weight dragged him down like a two-ton barbell. Every instinct he had screamed for him to stay as far away from this case—and as far away from this woman—as possible. He'd been through this grind before. A beautiful woman witness to a crime. A sad story. A need for his help. And him racing in on his white steed only to be bucked off. He'd be a fool to subject himself to that kind of torture again.

A fool or a masochist.

As if she could see the path his mind was traveling, she thrust her chin forward. "Listen, I can take care of myself. Just find out who murdered Win. We may not have had much of a relationship, but he was my husband. He deserves justice."

John pushed back from his desk and rose to his feet. The recliner and belt of Jack would have to wait because it didn't look like he was going home any time soon. "I'll look into it. But I'll need your permission to search the house. I want to bring in the county sheriff and a crime scene unit."

"Anything. I'll call Marcella, our housekeeper. She can let you in and give you any help you need."

"Good." The ache in his shoulders eased slightly. The evidence. All he had to do was trust the evidence. Trust the facts and leave feeling out of this. "I suggest you check into a hotel. At least until I can figure out what's going on."

Her head bobbed in a tight little nod. She was scared. Of that he was sure. And if someone had run her car into the Green Valley quarry as she claimed, she had damn good reason.

"If you let me know where you're staying, I'll ask the Madison police to keep an eye out." He gave her his best attempt at a reassuring smile. "You'll be okay."

ANDREA SLID the deadbolt home and followed it with the security chain. She'd been afraid a lot in her twenty-four years, but never as afraid as she was now.

She crossed the no-frills hotel room and lowered herself onto the bed. "Everything *is* going to be okay," she murmured to herself. "I'll survive this. I always do."

She'd faced the streets of Chicago alone at fifteen years old. She'd faced Wingate's temper alone. She'd faced the decision to leave him, even if she hadn't gotten the chance. She'd faced all of it and she'd survived. So far. But she'd never had someone trying to kill her. And worse yet, she'd never faced the loss of her memory—her very mind.

She glanced at the phone sitting on the nightstand. She wasn't totally alone. At least not as alone as she had been in that car last night. John Cohen had agreed to look into her story. He'd asked the Madison police to drive by the hotel and check on her. He'd promised to call as soon as he found anything.

When she'd first entered his office, she'd thought she was sunk. His dark intense eyes had seemed to drill right through her. His narrow face had seemed to harden against her, icy with cynicism. But as she told her story, she'd seen a transformation in him. Although he might still be skeptical, he'd listened. And when she'd finished explaining the unexplainable, he'd even seemed concerned. Far more than she'd gotten from another person in longer than she could remember.

And she still didn't know what to make of it.

She slipped her legs under the sheets and blanket and pulled the covers up to her shoulders, hoping the warmth would still the shaking in her bones. She had to keep her wits about her. She had to be strong. Because although John Cohen had offered to help, she knew better than to rely on him. Or anyone. And if an enemy of Wingate's had now set his sights on her, she might be up against more than she could handle this time.

Chapter Three

John sized up the man on the other side of the hand-shake. Even if Police Chief Gary Putnam wasn't dressed in blue, the average neighborhood thug would make him as a cop from a mile away. Close-cropped hair, wide shoulders, and slightly square demeanor, he was the kind of man the public trusted. The kind of cop John loved to put on the witness stand.

Andrea Kirkland's suspicions about the Green Valley police scrolled through his mind. If he was to pick a dirty cop—one who might want to silence the witness to a murder—Gary Putnam would be one of the last ones on his list.

Chief Putnam released the handshake and gestured John into his office. "Come in. It's quieter in here. We can talk."

John glanced over his shoulder at the tiny Green Valley police station. The place wasn't exactly a hub of activity. A young woman dressed in plain clothes hunched over an old typewriter, employing the hunt-and-peck method. Other than that, the place was quieter than a morgue.

John stepped into the office anyway and settled in a plastic-seated chair.

Not bothering to close the door, the chief sat behind a cheap-looking desk, the office furnishings of a public servant. "You want to know about Andrea Kirkland? Yes, she phoned last night. About dusk."

"And a woman named Ruth talked to her?"

"Yes. I was out on a call. Ruthie talked to Mrs. Kirkland just before she went home for the night." He nodded in the direction of the young woman typing. "She radioed me immediately. Mrs. Kirkland said her husband was missing."

"Did you check out her story?"

"I checked into it this morning. Very interesting situation."

"How so?"

"Seems no one has seen Wingate Kirkland for a week. Both his office in Madison and his company headquarters in Chicago were under the impression he was spending the time at his estate. Seems he's an avid deer hunter. The interesting part is that Mrs. Kirkland waited the entire week to report him gone."

Interesting indeed. Of course, there was a chance she was telling the truth about that, too. John had heard of instances where a person blocked a traumatic event from his or her mind only to have it surface later. "She says she must have blocked his death. That the memory didn't return until last night.''

''Is that what she says? She had amnesia or some damn thing? That's a new one. I guess it goes along with what she told Ruthie.''

''What did she tell Ruthie?''

''Ask her yourself.'' He glanced in the direction of the woman typing. ''What did Andrea Kirkland say to you last night, Ruthie?''

The typewriter quit tapping. John turned in his chair in time to see the young woman cross the office. Her shoulder-length hair was expertly styled. Her skin was flawless. And her clothing, though baggy and a lifeless brown color, was obviously expensive and ultimately tasteful. Ruthie dressed as though she was twenty going on fifty. ''She said she heard gunshots and saw Wingate lying on the floor. Anything else, she didn't remember.''

The chief focused his sharp eyes on Ruthie. ''And didn't she say something about an oriental rug?''

''A Persian rug,'' she corrected. ''She remembered seeing Mr. Kirkland's head resting on a Persian rug.''

That also squared with what she had told John. So far, so good.

Ruthie frowned slightly. ''The funny thing was, I saw a man loading a rug into a van in front of the Kirkland house about a week ago. I assumed Mrs. Kirkland was redecorating or having it cleaned.''

''When exactly did you see this?''

"Last Monday, I think. I remember because Mrs. Kirkland was outside giving the man directions."

A pain stabbed John's gut. The ulcer kicking up again. "Are you sure it was Mrs. Kirkland?"

"I think so. It's a long driveway. And the gate was closed. But there was a blond woman out there who looked like her. At least the way I remember Andrea Kirkland looking."

Not the most reliable witness testimony he'd heard. Not by a long shot. "You haven't seen Mrs. Kirkland in a while?"

"I'm afraid not. Even though I live next door, I haven't seen her very much. She keeps to herself."

"You live next door?" John tried to hide his surprise. The Wingate estate, a majestic old home Wingate Kirkland had restored and named after himself, was situated in a very exclusive rural development boasting one of the best views in Dane County. Although Ruthie's hair was tastefully cut and her wardrobe expensive, if staid, he wouldn't have pegged her for a member of the Kirkland's social set.

She dipped her head as if slightly embarrassed. "I still live with my parents. I'm Ruth Banks. My father is Gerald Banks."

"The judge?"

Ruthie smiled and nodded.

He knew Judge Banks well. The judge was notoriously tough on criminals. "Your father is a good man."

"Most prosecutors think so."

He smiled. The young woman was sharp. And the daughter of a judge would make a good witness. But from the sound of it, she didn't see much. Not enough to prove anything, at any rate. "Do you remember what the van looked like?"

"It was blue. Kind of light blue like a robin's egg."

"Did it have a company logo on the side?"

She pursed her lips in thought. "Yeah. I think it was yellow. Or gold. To tell you the truth, I didn't really pay attention."

A blue van with yellow or gold logo. At least it was something for the police to follow up. Provided Andrea Kirkland wasn't inventing the whole thing. A possibility he couldn't ignore. Not until a body turned up. "Can you think of any reason Andrea Kirkland would tell us her husband was murdered if it isn't true?"

Ruthie shook her head.

John glanced at Chief Putnam. "Can you, Chief?"

"You mean, why would she make it up?"

"If she did."

He shrugged his square shoulders. "Attention. Isn't that usually the thing? Maybe she's bored with her big house and charity events."

Was that the type of person Andrea Kirkland was? Even though John had only just met her, he couldn't buy it. "And if she is telling the truth? If her husband is dead?"

"Then I doubt we'll have to look any further than the obvious."

John had a pretty good idea of where he was leading, but he bit anyway. "What is the obvious?"

"That he was killed for his money. He sure has a lot of it. And rumor has it, Andrea Kirkland is the sole beneficiary of his will."

The ache returned to John's gut in force. Andrea was either making up the whole story, or she was the number-one suspect in a murder. Hell of a choice.

The bleat of his cell phone interrupted his thoughts. Excusing himself, he slipped out of the police chief's office, grabbed the phone off his belt and hit the talk button. "Yeah."

"Ace? It's Mylinski."

John grimaced at the nickname. Ever since an article praising his high conviction rate had run in the *State Journal*, Mylinski had latched onto the name. "Hey, Al." County Detective Al Mylinski was heading up the search of the Kirkland house. And despite his penchant for assigning stupid nicknames to nearly everyone he worked with, there was no one John trusted more. If there was anything to find, Al would sure as hell find it. "What do you have?"

"The LumaLite put on a really pretty light show."

John dragged in a deep breath. The LumaLite could show every trace of blood left at a crime scene, even when the blood wasn't visible to the naked eye. "Where?"

"Under the rug on the study floor."

"How much is there?"

"If someone cut himself, he needs more than a Band-Aid. There wasn't a drop on the rug, though. Someone replaced the rug and tried to clean the floor. If it wasn't for the LumaLite, we wouldn't have found anything."

"You didn't happen to notice a body lying around to make this easier on all of us, did you?"

"Sorry. But judging from the size of this pool of blood, there's a body out there somewhere. We'll start with the woods after we're finished with the house."

John blew out a gust of breath he didn't realize he was holding. At least one question was answered. Andrea didn't invent the story. But she sure as hell seemed to be neck-deep in it. He shouldn't be surprised. Like Putnam had said, start with the obvious. And the obvious in any murder was always the spouse.

He massaged the back of his neck and tried not to picture the graceful lines of Andrea Kirkland's face, her slender body, the desperation in her eyes. There was a reason cynicism ran rampant in all areas of law enforcement. Ninety-nine times out of a hundred it was warranted. And this case looked to be no different. Even if he wanted it to be.

"Gotta go. I'll keep my eyes open for that body, Ace."

"You do that, Al. You do that." John hit the button to cut off the call and clipped the phone back on his belt. If anyone had to keep his eyes open from here on out, it was him.

ANDREA PULLED OPEN the hotel room door and looked into the brown eyes of John Cohen. Relief eased through her, pushing aside the fear that had kept her wide awake all night.

He'd called her on his cell phone first thing this morning and told her he'd be right over. And even though she'd met the man only yesterday, she'd felt relieved to hear his voice. And to hear he had news about Wingate's murder, and she hoped the attack on her as well.

She swung the door wide. "Come in."

He ambled through the door on long legs, but his stride was anything but relaxed. His gaze darted around the room as if he expected to see a dead body secreted behind the Magic Fingers hotel bed or propped on the luggage rack in the closet.

Her mouth went dry. Whatever he'd discovered was worse than she'd feared. "Did you find Win? Is he dead?"

"No, we haven't found him. At least not yet. And as far as his condition, you'd probably know that better than anyone."

"Me?"

"Yes, you. You said you saw your husband's murder, didn't you?"

"I was hoping I was wrong. That it was all a bad dream or something." Her own words rang in her ears. She had been hoping exactly that. That her memories were a mistake. That Win was merely away on an unexpected business trip. That she could leave Wingate Estate and not look back.

But deep down she knew she'd been fooling herself. "Did you find something in the house?"

A muscle twitched along his jaw. "Yes. We did."

The shiver spread over her skin and settled in her bones. "What did you find?"

Instead of answering, he strode across the room, his long legs eating the distance in three strides. "You said you remembered your husband lying on a Persian rug after he was shot. What room was the rug in?"

She searched her memory. She could see the rug clearly. See Win's face contorting in pain. See the blood puddle underneath him like liquid tar soaking into silk. But she couldn't see anything else. "I'm not sure. We have a Persian rug in the dining room, the library and Win's study."

"Did you have any of those rugs replaced or cleaned since your husband disappeared?"

"No. They were just cleaned last spring. Why are you asking these things?"

"Because a neighbor of yours told me a man removed a Persian rug from your home and loaded it into a van only a week ago."

"That must have been him. That must have been the killer."

"Maybe. But my witness said one more thing."

"What?"

"That the man wasn't alone. That you were with him."

"Me?" Her pulse pounded in her ears. "I wasn't there. I couldn't have been."

He stared at her, his eyes boring past her defenses as if laying bare her jumbled thoughts.

She shuddered. "I didn't kill Wingate. I wouldn't. You've got to believe me."

John looked away, but it was too late. She could see the doubt play across his face, as plain as if he'd called her a liar.

He didn't believe her. The realization slammed into her like a kick to the stomach. She splayed her hands in front of her. "If I'd killed my husband, why would I call the police? Why would I come to you for help? Why would I tell you about the rug in the first place?"

"Questions I've been asking myself as well. And believe me, if not for the fact that the evidence fits your story—as far-fetched as that story seems—you'd be in custody right now."

"Custody?" The word chilled her blood like the biting November wind outside. "I'm telling the truth. Someone tried to kill me last night because of what I saw. What I remembered."

"Ah, yes. There's that. We have divers in the quarry looking for your car. Can we expect to find it?"

"Why wouldn't you?" Her voice sounded too shrill, too panicked.

A tired look descended into John Cohen's eyes.

Andrea cringed. *This* was the reaction he expected from her. Angry. Defensive. As if she was trying to hide something—trying to hide her husband's murder. She felt sick to her stomach. "Should I hire a lawyer?"

"Do you feel you need one?" His voice was a monotone. So different from the concerned note she'd convinced herself she'd heard yesterday. So different from what she wanted to hear. Needed to hear.

She shook her head. She hadn't killed Wingate. That was all there was to it. John Cohen's opinion shouldn't matter. It didn't matter. "No. I don't need one. I'm not guilty of anything. But I'm not sticking around for these accusations either." There was only one thing for her to do. What she'd planned to do all along—before Wingate's death, before she'd lost her memory, before she'd become the target of a killer in a black truck. She had to leave everything behind and start a new life.

A life where she would rely on no one but herself.

"Goodbye, Mr. Cohen. I should have known I wouldn't get any help from your office." Spinning on a heel, she strode from the room.

JOHN WATCHED Andrea retreat down the hotel's long hallway. Damn. Barely 8:00 a.m. and it had already been one hell of a day.

When he'd decided to come to her hotel, to confront her with what he'd learned, he'd been angry. Angry she'd lied to him. Angry she'd used him. And most of all, angry with himself for wanting to believe her when he knew damn well he'd be disappointed in the end.

But he'd come anyway. For some reason, he'd had to see her face when he confronted her with the story Ruthie Banks had told him. He had to look into her eyes and know she was hiding something. He had to know she was guilty.

But all he'd done was chase her out of the hotel before she'd told him anything.

Closing the hotel room door behind him, he started down the hall in the direction she'd gone. An elevator door chimed. He lengthened his stride, reaching Andrea's elevator just as the door closed.

He spotted the red exit sign and yanked open the stairwell door. Fluorescent lights hummed overhead, illuminating the stark stairs. He raced down the steps, his footfalls and breathing echoing against concrete. Reaching the bottom, he exploded into the lobby. Scanning the modest space, he spotted Andrea through the glass entry door.

She stood on the sidewalk looking over the nearly deserted parking lot, as if waiting for a ride. Her hair gleamed, clean and shiny, and flowed over her shoulders in a heavy blond wave. A far cry from the straggly mess he'd seen last night. And although the bruises still shadowed her jaw and hairline, the sunlight brought out a peach glow in her skin he'd thought could only be achieved with a cinematographer's artful lighting or the delicate touch of an airbrush.

Damn, she was an attractive woman. No wonder he'd wanted to believe her. If he had a brain left in his head, he'd turn this case over to Kit Ashner or some other rabid, female ADA in the office and stay as far away from Andrea Kirkland as possible.

Instead he crossed the lobby and pushed through the glass door. "Andrea."

She didn't turn around, as if she'd known he was watching her all along. "What do you want now?"

Good damn question. What did he want? For her to be innocent? For her to restore his faith in humanity? His faith in the value of his job? None of those things were going to happen.

Then why was he here? "I want to ask you a few more questions."

"Why? So you can prove I murdered my husband? So you can throw me in jail?"

"Only if you're guilty."

"Well, I'm not."

"Then answer my questions."

She plunked hands on hips in a show of strength. But despite her bravado, he could see her hands shake. "Maybe I *should* get myself a lawyer."

He gestured to the parking lot. "Fine. Do you have

one in mind? I'll give you a ride to his office. It'll save me a trip later."

Her bravado faltered, and suddenly she was shaking all over. Tears glittered in the corners of her eyes. She blinked, the moisture spiking her lashes. "Please, leave me alone."

"I can't do that." Oh hell. If there was anything he hated, it was making a woman cry. Especially a woman like Andrea Kirkland. Unless it was all an act, of course. God knew some women could summon crocodile tears every time they needed to weasel out of a speeding ticket. But somehow he couldn't deny the feeling that Andrea Kirkland wasn't one of them. "Listen, your husband was a bastard. It sounds like he was asking for whatever he got. Maybe he tried to hit you. Maybe you killed him in self defense."

"It didn't happen that way. I was leaving him. I didn't kill him."

"Maybe you didn't do it yourself. Maybe someone else got out of hand. Maybe you never intended for your husband to die."

She shook her head, her hair sweeping across one eye. "I didn't kill Wingate. I didn't help anyone kill Wingate."

"But you don't remember. Who's to say—"

"I don't need to remember. I never could have hurt Wingate. I never could have hurt anyone." She closed her eyes. When she opened them, tears spiked her lashes with moisture. "I'm waiting for a cab. Please let me wait in peace."

He shook his head, a last-ditch effort. "Cabs take forever to arrive in this city. I have a car. Why don't you let me drive you?"

"I'll take a bus." She stepped past him and into the parking lot.

Rubber screeched on pavement. A pickup circled the corner of the hotel. A black Dodge with tinted windows. It accelerated, its engine roaring.

And shot straight for Andrea.

John raced across the sidewalk and onto the asphalt. Into the truck's path. "Andrea!"

She turned to the sound of his voice and spotted the truck. Her eyes widened.

The truck closed the distance in a heartbeat.

John lunged for her, lowering his shoulders. He hit her full force, pushing her to the pavement between two cars just as the truck rifled past.

Chapter Four

The roar of the truck's engine fading, John struggled to catch his breath. There was no doubt in his mind that the driver had been gunning for Andrea. Trying to kill her. He rolled his weight off her. Wiping thick blond hair back from her cheek, he tried to see her face, to make sure she was all right. She had to be all right. "Andrea?"

Her eyes opened. Drawing in a deep breath, she pushed into a sitting position and scraped the remaining strands out of her eyes. Her injured hand left a trail of crimson on one cheek. "The truck— Did you see?" A strangled sound erupted from deep in her throat. The unmistakable sound of fear.

"It almost ran you down."

"It was the same. The same truck that ran me off the road and into the quarry."

John gritted his teeth, fighting the urge to wrap her in his arms, to comfort her. There was no time. The truck could be back any moment. And this time he had the feeling the driver would make sure he didn't miss. He pointed to a full-sized silver van towering above the cars. "My car is just on the other side of that van. Do you think you can make it?"

She swallowed hard, as if pushing down her panic. "I can make it."

"Good. Lean on me if you need to." He held out a hand.

She grasped it. Her hand trembled. Her palm was sticky, blood oozing from raw flesh. She pressed her lips together in a determined line and nodded. "Let's go."

Rising to a crouch, John peered over the trunk of one of the cars. The distant roar of a truck engine cut through the still air. He looked in the direction of the sound, waiting for the black behemoth to appear from around the corner and crash headlong into the parked cars, pinning them between the twisted metal. But he couldn't spot the sound's source. The parking lot was still as death.

Time to make their move. He pulled her up. Still crouched, he dodged through the maze of cars, Andrea on his heels. Reaching his blue sedan, he unlocked the driver's door and motioned her inside.

She scrambled over the stick shift and into the passenger seat. John ducked behind the wheel. He slipped the key in the ignition and turned it. The engine revved to life.

Suddenly the sound of the engine grew louder, deeper as it was joined by another engine's growl.

Andrea gasped. "The truck."

"Hold on." Throwing the car in reverse, John hit the gas. The car shot backward. He yanked the wheel to one side. Tires screeching, it spun in place.

And faced the truck.

Black windows stared like malevolent eyes. The front bumper was dented. The perfect gleam of the truck's right fender was marred by silver paint. No doubt the color of Andrea's car.

She covered her mouth, stifling a scream.

John hit the gas. The car leaped forward. Another twist of the wheel and his car dodged to the side, just missing a black fender. He pressed his foot to the floor. He took the corner full throttle, tires screeching in protest. Fishtailing out of the parking lot, they raced onto the highway frontage road.

One eye on the rearview mirror, John tried to steady his pulse. The black truck was nowhere to be seen, as if it and its driver had disappeared.

"No one is following. It looks like we lost him."

Andrea stared shell-shocked at the cars around them, as if she was convinced any one of them might morph into the black truck at any moment. "You believe me now?" Her voice rang hollow, mono-toned.

He'd seen the evidence with his own eyes. The black truck. The squeal of rubber as it shot straight for Andrea. "Do I believe someone is trying to kill you? Yes."

"And Wingate? Do you still think I killed him?"

He blew a breath through tight lips. He'd gone to her hotel room this morning to catch her in a lie, to prove she'd killed her husband, and to banish her from his mind for good. But instead of getting answers, he was stuck with more questions and no convincing evidence. He didn't even have a body. "I don't know."

"I suppose that's an improvement. Maybe if the truck had run me down, you'd actually believe me."

Maybe I believe you now.

He clamped down on the thought. A bitter laugh lodged in his throat. Hadn't he seen enough in his years in the district attorney's office to know how easily people lie? Didn't he know the lengths people would go to protect their own guilty hides?

He damn well should. But somehow, when he saw the tears in Andrea's eyes, when he heard the fear and sincerity in her voice, he forgot every hard lesson the past fifteen years had taught.

Whether she was guilty of killing her husband or not, he *wanted* to believe her. And that scared him more than a charging black truck ever could.

STILL TREMBLING, Andrea stood in front of the window in John Cohen's cramped office. She felt like a sitting duck waiting for the bullet. She hadn't wanted

to come here. She hadn't wanted to report the latest
incident with the black truck to the police. She'd
wanted to disappear, to get out of town. She'd be
long gone if that truck hadn't shown up.

And she'd be dead if John Cohen hadn't pushed
her out of the way.

She shook her head. It didn't make sense. John
Cohen had bullied her, accused her and refused to
believe her. But he hadn't hesitated to rush into on-
coming traffic to save her life.

She turned away from the window and raked her
gaze over his office. The battered desk. The ancient
chairs. The stacks of files that towered like pine trees
in the north woods. With most people, she could get
a sense of them by examining their surroundings. Not
so John Cohen. The room was so plain, so devoid of
personality, the only feeling she could glean from it
was the bone-deep ache of fatigue.

And a loneliness that spoke to something in her
own soul.

She shook her head and wrapped her arms around
herself. Ridiculous. She didn't know John Cohen,
and she didn't want to know him. She wanted to get
out of this office. She wanted to get as far away from
the police and the district attorney as she could. She
wanted to disappear.

Male voices filtered in from the hallway. John
pushed the door wide and strode inside alone. He
crossed to his desk and dropped a small stack of files

on the already heaped desktop. "I struck out. Seems the department doesn't have the man hours available to offer citizens protection from what they consider to be two unfortunate accidents."

She breathed a sigh of relief. "I told you I didn't want the cops involved."

He frowned. "Because you still think the Green Valley police are after you?"

"You might not want to take a chance either if your life was on the line."

He held up his hands as if trying to fend off her anger. "You've got to admit, that's a hard one to swallow."

"All I know is that I called the Green Valley police station and the next thing I knew, the black truck was after me." She paced to the far side of the office, shaking her head. "You know what? It doesn't matter. I'll take care of myself when it comes to the black truck."

He narrowed his eyes on her. "And how do you propose to do that?"

"I can get lost. I've done it before."

"Not when you're involved in a murder investigation, you haven't."

"I've told you everything I know."

"Which is close to nothing."

"It's all I remember."

"You can't just throw half memories and paranoia

out there and then 'get lost' as you say. Especially not when you're a suspect.''

She bit the inside of her cheek. Her story probably did sound like half memories and paranoia to him. It sure sounded that way to her, and she'd lived through it. A bubble of helplessness rose in her throat. She might have never quite had control of her life, but she'd always had control of her memories.

Now she'd lost even that.

She straightened her spine and forced herself to meet his dark eyes. She couldn't afford to be helpless. She couldn't afford to be weak. Not now. Not ever again. ''What about hypnosis? I've heard of lost memories being retrieved under hypnosis.''

He shook his head. ''Can't do it. You may be the only witness to a murder. Hypnosis introduces questions about which memories are real and which are planted. Once you go under hypnosis your testimony is worthless in a court of law.''

''So what do I do?'' She swallowed, trying to keep the panic at bay. She could make a run for it, but somehow the image of her dashing down the hall with John Cohen on her heels was too ridiculous to contemplate. Judging from his runner's physique, he'd probably catch her before she made it to the office door.

He let out a long, defeated sigh. ''You mean, what do *we* do?''

She looked at him hard. ''We?''

"If you think I'm going to have a relaxing week-end chugging beer, watching football and waiting to read about your death in Sunday's *State Journal,* guess again."

A chill prickled over her skin. "What are you say-ing?"

"I'm saying that you're stuck with me. Until we get some answers about this case or I can convince the police to spring for an officer to keep an eye on you, I'm your bodyguard. And your personal mem-ory coach."

"Oh no, you're not."

"Do you have any other ideas?"

"Yes. You find out who killed Wingate and I leave."

"Try again."

"I'll go someplace safe and give you a number where I can be reached."

He shook his head. "You're either my key witness or my prime suspect. Either way, I'm not letting you out of my sight."

She glanced at the door. Maybe she should recon-sider running for it, just throw open the door and dash down the hall. Maybe it was her only chance to get out of this mess.

Ridiculous.

But equally ridiculous was the idea of John as her bodyguard. No, not ridiculous. Dangerous. Because even now, with his questions and threats still ringing in her ears, she could hear the loneliness in his voice. And she could feel her heart respond.

"You can wipe that scared rabbit look off your face. I'm not going to hurt you, for God's sake. I'm going to keep you safe."

She didn't know if he intended to hurt her or not, but she did know that being around him certainly wouldn't keep her safe. "And what can I say to change your mind?"

"Nothing. But there's something you can do."

"What?"

"If you didn't murder your husband, prove it. Help me find who did."

She gnawed on the inside of her cheek until she raised a sore. If they found the real murderer, if they put him behind bars, she would be safe. Both from the killer trying to prevent her from remembering and from the police trying to pin Win's murder on her. All she had to do was stay strong a little longer. Because a little longer and she'd be away from John Cohen for good. "What do you want me to do?"

"You can start by going with me to see a man about a rug."

JOHN GLANCED at Andrea standing next to him in the showroom of Ryman International Rugs and took a deep breath. A light scent tickled his nose. Floral and feminine. The kind of scent that caused a man to lose his mind.

Too late for him. He'd obviously already lost what little gray matter he'd had rattling in his skull. That was the only explanation for what he was doing, playing bodyguard to a woman who could be a murderess. And, even worse, playing Holmes to her Watson.

He massaged the aching muscles in his neck while pretending to examine the multi-colored silk of one of the elaborate Persian rugs hanging from the ceiling. On the drive across town, he'd told himself he was just doing his job, just trying to keep her safe. Well, she might be safe, but he sure wasn't sane. Not around her. Her body had him as hot and humid as a Wisconsin July. And every time she looked at him with those bruised eyes of hers, he had the feeling he had the power to make things better.

Or at least he'd go down trying.

He needed to get the hell away from her. And he needed to start by finding some answers about who killed Wingate Kirkland. And whether the woman beside him was a suspect or a witness.

"Hello there. I'm Oscar Ryman. Can I help you find a certain type of rug?"

John spun around and looked into the man's bespeckled eyes. He'd tracked the blue van with the gold logo to Ryman International Rugs, a small rug shop on Madison's upscale west side. Oscar Ryman must be the owner. He held his identification out for the man to examine. "I'm with the district attorney's office, and I need to ask you a few questions about a rug.''

"The district attorney's office, huh? Is this about a crime?'' Tall and wire-thin, Ryman nearly quivered with excitement. Apparently the rug business lacked drama. If he only knew the reality of life in the district attorney's office, he'd see what a real lack of drama was like.

John fixed him with his best all-business stare. If this guy wanted to pretend he was a bit player on "Law and Order," John had no problem going along. Especially since guys like this were willing to turn themselves inside out to provide information. ''A week ago, one of your trucks picked up a rug at Wingate Estate—''

"Out in Green Valley, right? A Persian. Top-of-the-line. But you're mistaken. We didn't pick it up. We delivered it.''

"You delivered a new rug and picked up a stained one?''

He tilted his head to one side as if doing so would connect normally unused synapses. "I don't think there was a pick-up with that order.''

"Can you check?''

"Certainly.'' He spun around and almost skipped to the tall desk looming in the center of the sales floor. At least John didn't have to worry about this one hiding anything from him. On the contrary, this guy would probably be calling him all next week with meaningless details he remembered about the transaction.

John followed him. Once he had been that eager to prosecute the bad guys and lock them behind bars, that eager to make a difference in the world. Ages had passed since then.

Andrea stepped up next to him at the desk and leaned close, trying to see the manager's computer screen.

Awareness prickled John's skin like static electricity. Forcing himself to step a safe distance away, he peered over the manager's shoulder. Dates, numbers and names were arranged in neat columns on the computer screen.

"Here it is," the man pointed at the screen. "Wingate Kirkland, delivery. If there had been a pick-up, it would be noted here."

Maybe Ruthie Banks was mistaken. Maybe she hadn't seen Ryman's delivery van hauling away a rug. Maybe she'd seen them delivering it.

Or maybe the computer wasn't telling the whole story. "Who was the employee who delivered the rug?"

The manager squinted down at the screen. "Sutcliffe. Hank Sutcliffe."

"Where can I find Mr. Sutcliffe?"

Ryman shrugged his bony shoulders. "Can't help you, I'm afraid. Sutcliffe quit last week."

Damn. Just his luck. Now he'd have to track the man down. "What day did he quit?"

"Monday. Didn't even give two weeks notice. In fact, his last delivery was the one you're asking about. The one to Wingate Estate."

"Do you have a forwarding address for him?"

"Afraid not. He said he was moving back to Chicago, but he didn't leave an address."

Damn. The lack of a forwarding address would make the job of tracking him down tougher. Not impossible, but more time-consuming. "Where are you going to send his last paycheck?"

"He told me to keep my money. Said he didn't need it. So unless he changes his mind and comes to collect the check, I'm taking him at his word."

Interesting. Doubtful a man who worked delivering rugs made so much money he didn't need his last paycheck. Unless he'd come into a lot of money from another source.

A source that paid him to haul away a blood-soaked rug.

John glanced at Andrea. She watched Ryman, her gaze steady, open, as if she had nothing to hide.

Or was that just what he wanted to see?

Ryman popped his head up from the computer. "I do have a picture of him."

"A picture?" John glanced at Andrea again. A picture might be helpful for jogging her memory. "Can I see it?"

The manager reached for a stack of glossy advertising flyers balanced on the edge of the desk. Grabbing a flyer, he gave it to John. "Here he is, carrying the rug."

The flyer was an ad for free rug delivery and pick-up with cleaning or purchase. In the center of the photo, a beefy blond Adonis grinned at the camera, his trunk-like arms wrapped around a rolled rug. He handed the advertisement to Andrea. "Recognize him?"

A crease dug into her forehead. Releasing a breath, her face fell. "I'm sorry."

John fought the need to trace a finger over the lines of frustration tooled in her forehead and around her mouth. As if he could erase them. As if he could make things better for her with the touch of his hand.

He forced himself to turn back to Ryman. If the man had sold the rug to Andrea, he would have recognized her when she walked in the door. But *someone* must have bought the rug. "Do your records show who bought the rug?"

"You mean who placed the order?"

"Who picked it out, who placed the order, who paid for it."

"I picked it out."

"You did?"

He bobbed his head. "I'm an interior designer by trade. Many of our clients leave the selection of their rugs up to me. The client just tells me his or her ideas for the room and I do the rest.''

"Then who placed the order?''

He peered up from the computer screen, his eyes distorted through his thick lenses. "Why Mr. Kirkland, of course.''

"Mr. Kirkland?''

Andrea's head whipped around. Her gaze latched onto his. The same surprise emanated from her eyes as he knew was in his own.

Out of all the names the man could have uttered, that was the one John expected least. It was impossible. If the rug was replaced to hide the blood from Kirkland's murder, how could Kirkland have ordered it himself? "Are you sure it was just last week?''

"Of course. I don't make my exceptional clients wait.''

"And you're sure you talked to Wingate Kirkland?''

"I didn't take the order. I believe Hank Sutcliffe did.'' He tapped the computer screen with a fingernail. "Yes. Here's his name. And on the invoice there's a note that Mr. Kirkland called from his Chicago office and wanted the rug delivered ASAP and billed to his business, Kirkland Development in Chicago.''

The rug order was placed from Kirkland's business in Chicago. The man replacing the rug had disappeared to Chicago—the very man who'd taken the order. It seemed the answers John needed were in Chicago.

A pain stabbed his gut. He reached into his pocket for his antacids and popped a couple into his mouth. He knew what he should do. Call Detective Mylinski, give him the information and let him handle the Chicago connection when he dug up the time.

If only it could be that easy.

But someone was after Andrea Kirkland, someone who wanted her dead. He couldn't afford to wait until Mylinski could find the time. He needed answers now. He had to go to Chicago. And there wasn't a chance in hell he could leave Andrea Kirkland home alone.

Chapter Five

Andrea looked out the wall of glass flanking one side of Kirkland Development's lobby and shivered. The office overlooked South Wabash, a block from South Michigan Avenue and the skeletons of leafless trees swaying in Grant Park. Lake Michigan peered between buildings, a sliver of steely blue pocked with whitecaps. The interior of the office suite was a study in state-of-the-art glass-and-chrome decor. As cold as the wind whipping outside.

She turned away from the view and glanced at John. She'd been surprised when he'd announced they were going to Chicago to check on the rug dealer's story. Heck, she'd been shocked. So shocked she hadn't thought to resist. The only thing she'd considered was finding Win's killer. She hadn't taken the effect of a road trip with John into account. Not until she'd been in the close confines of his car for the two-and-a-half-hour interstate drive.

Not that they'd touched on any intimate subjects

on the drive down. Not unless what little she knew about Wingate's wide array of business investments could be considered intimate. But although the topic was relatively safe, the way John had watched her and listened to her made her feel as if she was trusting him with her deepest secrets. As if they were forging some kind of bond.

She squirmed in the plush reception-room chair. She couldn't let herself think that way, feel that way. She'd been weak when she'd met Wingate. She had to be strong now. She had to go it alone. And that meant she had to be on her guard around John Cohen.

At the sound of her movement, John's gaze found hers. "What is it?"

She looked away. "I was just thinking about Wingate," she lied. "About what Ryman said."

"That your husband ordered the rug?"

"Yes. Hank Sutcliffe must have mistaken Win's voice."

"That or he lied about it." John glanced around the office. "Did your husband order a lot of rugs?"

"He has—*had* a number of personal properties, but I wouldn't say he's ordered a lot of rugs for them."

"How about for Kirkland Development property?"

She choked back a laugh. "You're kidding, right?"

"Kidding? Why?"

"His properties in Madison are upscale, but that's not where he got his start. He may have liked to call himself a real-estate baron, but slum lord was more like it."

"The places he owns are that nice, huh?"

Her windpipe constricted as if squeezed by an invisible hand. She didn't want to think about the rundown apartment buildings Wingate owned or the people who were forced to live in that squalor. Desperate women. Fatherless children. Teenage boys looking for a place to belong. And teenage girls searching for a way out. "Yeah. That nice."

"How long has it been since you've been here?"

"To this office?"

"Yes."

"I've never been here."

He raised his brows. "Never?"

"Wingate never invited me. He kept his business and personal lives separate. Not that I was clamoring to visit. I've never had much of a head for business."

"I get the impression you could do anything you want to. Including making a business success of yourself."

Despite the cold surroundings, warmth kindled inside her at his words. She tried to douse the spark. "It would be nice to think so."

"Then think so," he said. "Because I mean it."

She could feel John's gaze move over her face,

heat smoldering where it touched. She shifted in her chair, careful not to look in his eyes.

"Assistant District Attorney Cohen?"

He looked up. Shoving himself to his feet, he thrust his hand toward the woman with short red hair and guarded eyes. "Ms. Graham?"

"Yes," Ramona Graham, the office administrator, confirmed. She shook his hand. "The receptionist said you have some questions?"

"Yes."

She gave Andrea a dismissive glance, as if deciding she was merely John's assistant and not worth the bother of a handshake. "I don't have much time, but I'll do my best to answer. Follow me." She spun on a high heel and bustled past the reception desk and into a catacomb of offices. Taking a sharp corner, she led them into a spacious office with a million-dollar view of the lake.

Once inside the office, Ramona hunkered down behind the large marble-topped desk that dominated the room as if retreating into a foxhole. She gave John a bullet-proof smile. "Now, how can I help you?"

Sitting in a white leather chair, Andrea faced the desk. John lowered himself into the chair next to her. "When was the last time you talked to Wingate Kirkland?"

"He was in the office two weeks ago."

"And you haven't talked to him since? On the phone? E-mail?"

"No. He always takes a couple of weeks off in November. He's an avid deer hunter. Both rifle and bow hunting. And this year with the expanded hunting season, I assume he's decided to take even more time. Have you tried reaching him at Wingate Estate?"

"Yes."

She pursed her lips and twisted them to the side. "He might be on a hunting trip. With chronic wasting disease affecting the deer in southern Wisconsin, maybe he went out of state this year."

Andrea tangled her fingers together in her lap. Win's office administrator seemed to know more about Win's comings and goings than she did. Not a surprise. Andrea hadn't known her husband for a long time. Maybe she'd never really known him.

"What did you say this was about?" Ramona Graham glanced at her watch, a reminder she was a busy woman.

"I didn't say." John set his briefcase on his lap, opened it and pulled out the glossy flyer he'd gotten from the rug dealer. Holding it up for Ramona's inspection, he pointed to the picture of Sutcliffe. "Do you know this man?"

She slipped on a pair of gold reading glasses. Her lips flattened into a straight line. "No. I can't say I do." Slipping the glasses off, she dropped them, letting them swing on the chain around her neck. "Is there anything else?"

Whether Ramona Graham was hiding something or really didn't recognize Hank Sutcliffe, Andrea didn't know. It didn't matter. Even if John pressed her, it wouldn't do any good. No doubt her job as Wingate's gatekeeper had made her good at burying skeletons. And keeping them in the ground.

Apparently John recognized that fact as well. "There is something else. Do you know if someone here ordered a rug for the Kirkland home about a week ago?"

"A rug?" A furrow struggled to appear between Ramona's brows. "I could check. Was it for the Chicago apartment, the Wisconsin cabin, Wingate Estate, or the Florida house?"

John glanced at Andrea as if tallying up the extent of her inheritance.

She tried to hide her cringe. With riches like that, no wonder he and everyone else thought she was after Win's money. But what John didn't understand was that she'd give it all up tomorrow never to have succumbed to her insecurities and married Wingate in the first place.

John turned back to Ramona. "Wingate Estate."

She gave a nod and bustled out the office door. When she returned, she held a folder in front of her. "It appears no order for furnishings of any kind has been made since these offices were redecorated several months ago.''

Redecorated? Andrea eyed the glass-and-chrome decor. Who had they hired as a designer? Jack Frost? She shouldn't be surprised. The cold interior fit the Wingate she'd come to know to a T.

"Maybe Mrs. Kirkland ordered the rug,'' Ramona offered. Andrea glanced at John. Little did Ramona know that Mrs. Kirkland was sitting right in front of her.

John met her gaze for a second before returning his attention to Ramona. "Maybe I could call Mrs. Kirkland and ask her.''

Ramona nodded as if to encourage him, anything as long as he let her get back to her important business. "She's probably the one who placed the order. I'm sure she'll be able to help.''

"Do you know where Mrs. Kirkland is staying?'' John asked.

"I believe she's at the John Hancock building apartment. I haven't spoken to her since she stopped in last week.''

Shock ripped through Andrea. "She stopped in last week? Mrs. Kirkland? Are you sure?''

Ramona frowned at Andrea as if she'd lost her mind. "Yes, I'm quite sure. She has been here many times with Mr. Kirkland. Now, if we're finished, I have some urgent business to attend to.'' Ramona stood and stretched out her hand over the desk.

John and Andrea both rose. Turning his attention to Ramona, John shook the hand she offered. ''Thank you for your time.'' Cupping Andrea's elbow, he steered her out the office door and down the hall to the reception area.

Andrea stared straight ahead as she walked, numbness giving way to disbelief. Damn Wingate. If someone had told her he'd be able to hurt her even more after all she'd been through, she wouldn't have believed it. But somehow, the realization that he was having an affair right under her nose cut her just as surely as if she actually cared.

The warmth of John's hand on her arm seeped into her. Learning her husband had had an affair was bad enough without having John find out along with her. If there were times curling up and dying were preferable to taking another breath, this was certainly one of them.

They stepped out of the office suite and into the hallway. As soon as Kirkland Development's door swung closed behind them, John turned to face her. Even though the sun streaming in through the window behind him cast a shadow over his eyes, she knew he was looking straight through her. Seeing her hurt. Her weakness. ''For what it's worth, I'm sorry.''

She cringed. ''For what? Did you introduce Wingate and the woman passing as Mrs. Kirkland? Or did you force him to set up house with her? No, don't tell me. You must have forced me to shuck my self-respect and marry the bastard in the first place.''

''You have the right to be angry. Damned angry.'' A corner of his mouth quirked into a half grin. ''I like seeing a little fight in your eyes. It's a hell of a lot better than those damned bruises.''

''Bruises?'' Her fingers automatically flew to the tender spot along her jaw where her chin had hit the steering wheel of her Lexus.

''Figurative bruises.'' He raised a hand to her face and skimmed a finger along her cheekbone. ''You deserve better. Much better.''

Warmth skittered along her skin at his touch. She expelled a breath through tight lips, her indignation going with it. She looked at the gray carpet, at the bank of elevators, at anything but John's face. But no matter how she tried to shield herself, she could feel those piercing brown eyes penetrate her defenses and peer into her soul.

She sucked in a breath. ''For the record, I didn't know about the other Mrs. Kirkland. Not until today.''

''I know.''

''How do you know?''

''I see guilty defendants all the time. I cross-examine them. I gauge their weaknesses and try to rip them apart. I'm far from figuring you out, but I do know that Ramona's bombshell was a surprise.''

He trailed his finger down her cheek and brushed her hair back behind her ear.

Shivers marauded over her skin. She raised her gaze to meet his, as if pulled by a magnet.

She wanted to trust him. Wanted to rely on him. Wanted to give in to the loneliness building inside her like a physical ache.

If only she didn't have to lose herself in the process.

"So what happens now?" She forced the question past her lips, though she knew what his answer would be.

He paused for a long time, as if weighing the options. When he finally spoke, his voice was low and rough. "We talk to the other Mrs. Kirkland."

JOHN WELCOMED the hard cold slap of the Chicago wind as he and Andrea reached the sidewalk outside Kirkland Development. Maybe the wind could smack some sense into him. God knew he wasn't doing a good job of getting a grip on his own.

He never should have touched Andrea. Never should have stroked her satin cheek. Never should have fingered the heavy silk of her hair. Now, not only did he have to fight the look of need and vulnerability in her eyes, he had the memory of caressing her knocking around in his head. And tempting him to do it again.

Before they reached the parking ramp where he'd

stowed his car, the bleat of his cell phone cut through the noise of traffic and his jumbled thoughts. He slipped the phone from his belt, hit the talk button and held it to his ear. "Yeah."

"I missed you in your office today, Ace. It's not like you to take an afternoon off." Al Mylinski's voice boomed over the phone.

"I'm not taking it off, Al. Trust me. What's up?"

"I'm at the Green Valley police station. I just left the Kirkland place."

"Tell me you've found a body."

"No such luck. Not yet, anyway. But we found something." Al paused dramatically in that maddening way of his.

"Cut the suspense, Al."

"So it's working?"

"Spill it."

"There was a gun hidden in one of the fireplaces. A Ruger SP100. It's registered to Kirkland himself. It was fired recently. Could be the murder weapon. Can't tell until we find a body with wounds to match. I'm heading back out to the estate now. The dogs should arrive any time to start searching the grounds."

John's mind spun with possible implications. "An SP100?"

"Yep. It's a smaller-framed version of their GP100. Just the right size for a woman's hand. And that brings me to the rest of the reason I'm calling."

"What's that?"

"Seems Andrea Kirkland has gone missing. She never checked out of her hotel, just left."

John glanced at Andrea walking beside him. "I know."

"Any idea where she went?"

"She's fine. She's with me."

Andrea's gaze flicked to him. If she had any questions about whom he was discussing, she had no reason to wonder now.

"Damn it, John." Mylinski's voice roared over the phone. "What the Sam heck do you think you're doing?"

"Someone's trying to kill her, Al. I was there this morning. A truck tried to run her over. I'm guessing it's the same truck that put her car at the bottom of Green Valley quarry. She needs protection."

"And *you're* going to protect her from this truck? How?"

"I figure I'll throw a law book at the windshield. Or threaten to sue."

Mylinski let out a bark of laughter. "Joking aside, you might need protection from her more than she needs it from you. If Kirkland's dead, she's the number-one suspect."

"Another reason to keep an eye on her."

"Just so you're careful. You don't want to relive the past."

John glanced at Andrea out of the corner of his

eye. He might believe someone was trying to kill her. He might even hope she was innocent. But he wasn't about to forget she could be a murderer. And he wasn't going to relive past mistakes. "Not a chance." The el roared and screeched on the tracks overhead, drowning out his words.

"Ace?" Mylinski yelled in John's ear. "It sounds like you're in the middle of a steel mill. Where are you, anyway?"

"Chicago."

"You took her out of state?" John could hear Mylinski's teeth grinding over the phone. Either that or he was munching those damn candies he never seemed to be without.

"She's not going anywhere."

"Even so, you know how this is going to look. Damn it, John, after that last thing, you'd better hope Dex Harrington doesn't find out about this."

"Dex? He's still celebrating his reelection as district attorney after that Andrew Clarke Smythe mess."

"You'd better hope so."

John fished a roll of antacids from the pocket of his overcoat, popped several in his mouth and tried not to look in Andrea's direction. "We'll be back in Madison tonight, Al. And I intend to bring a few answers with me."

"I hope they're good answers, Ace. Good enough to cover your ass."

So did he. For his own sake—and for Andrea's.

JOHN WATCHED lighted numbers flash over the elevator door. His ears popped with the change in altitude as he and Andrea rode to the upper floors of the John Hancock Building. He tried not to look at her, standing so close in the confined space. If he did, he'd only want to lean toward her, to draw in her fragrance, to touch the silk of her hair once again.

It wasn't her looks that lured him in—though God knew, she was attractive as hell. It wasn't even the intelligence sparkling in her eyes. It was something else. Her vulnerability, maybe. Or the way she looked at him, as if she believed he could fix her problems, as if she believed he could make a difference.

The elevator door slid open, and they stepped out. His shoes sank into carpet the color of fresh cream. Cream-on-cream patterned wallpaper graced the walls, punctuated by gold-framed artwork, mirrors and console tables laden with fresh flower arrangements.

Nice digs. He tried to picture Andrea living in a place like this. Dressed to the nines for a night on the town. Busying herself with her pet charities while her husband worked long hours. Polishing her nails so she would look beautiful for him while he was setting up house with another woman.

It made him sick.

"This is it." Andrea eyed the white, paneled door as if it might bite, and made no move to knock.

He couldn't blame her for not wanting to face what was on the other side of that door. When he'd told her he didn't like seeing the bruises in her eyes, that he preferred her angry, he'd meant it. He'd seen victims every day of his professional life. He didn't want to see her as one.

Almost as much as he didn't want to see her as a murderer.

He rapped on the door.

A brunette with large dark eyes peered out into the hall. Though the woman had to be even younger than Andrea, she had a brittleness about her that only came with hard living and meanness. The corners of her red lips dipped.

John pulled identification from his wallet and held it up for her inspection. "I'm John Cohen from the district attorney's office in Dane County, Wisconsin. The office manager at Kirkland Development said you were staying here, Mrs. Kirkland."

The red lips quirked upward into a snide smile. "Don't bother with the Mrs. Kirkland bull. I know who she is." She narrowed her eyes on Andrea.

"Then the question is, who are you?"

"I don't suppose you'd believe I'm Win's long-lost cousin."

John gave her a look. "Not a chance."

She shrugged, as if she didn't care. But the move-

ment was tense and forced. "I'm Tonnie. Tonnie
Bartell. Take your questions to Wingate. He can explain everything." She stepped back, ready to shut
the door.

John stuck the toe of his shoe between door and
frame. "I suggest you talk to me. This is part of a
criminal investigation."

The door stopped mid arc. "Criminal investigation? I'm not doing anything wrong."

He didn't have time to get into the things she was
doing wrong. "Then you won't mind cooperating.
When was the last time you saw Wingate Kirkland?"

"I don't know."

"Ramona Graham said you visited Kirkland Development's office a week ago."

"What of it? Win and I had talked about going to
dinner. Is that a crime?"

"Ramona said he wasn't there."

Tonnie forced a shrug. "He must have decided to
leave early."

"To go to Wingate Estate?"

She glanced at Andrea, her eyes shooting bullets.
"He hunts deer."

John looked from Tonnie to Andrea and back
again. Not only did Tonnie know who Andrea was,
she obviously didn't like her. Each glance screamed
dislike loud and clear. A dislike John might be able
to use to blast out the truth. "Instead of keeping his

dinner plans with you, he went to Wisconsin to be with his wife?''

''Is that what she told you? I suppose she also said she pined away until her Prince Charming came back to the castle. What a laugh.'' She homed in on Andrea. ''You might be able to fool Mr. District Attorney, but you can't fool me. Win told me all about you.''

Andrea's eyes narrowed.

''He told me you married him for his money, how you made him change his will.''

Andrea's lips thinned into a bloodless line. ''I didn't make him do anything.''

''That's not what I heard. He said you threatened to divorce him if he didn't agree to leave everything to you.''

Andrea glanced up at John. ''I never threatened Wingate. Believe me, it was the other way around.''

''At first I thought he was doing it just to keep money-grubbing sister Joyce from getting her hooks into his dough,'' Tonnie continued. ''But it seems there's more than one money grubber in his life. Only you make Joyce seem generous by comparison.''

John watched Tonnie. There was a lot of anger there. Anger and self-delusion. It didn't take much imagination to see little Miss Mistress following her precious Win up to his estate and confronting him about standing her up. And if a gun was handy…

If he only knew in which house Kirkland usually kept the gun Mylinski found. If it was usually in Chicago, John might have something to give Mylinski. Not much, but it beat returning empty-handed. "Does Kirkland keep a gun here?"

"A gun?" She narrowed her eyes again, this time on John. "What kind of criminal investigation is this? Is Win in some kind of trouble?"

"We don't know. But unless you want take the risk of being in trouble right along with him, you'd better answer the question." He glanced down the hall at the woman peeking out her apartment door. "And if you don't want your neighbors to know all about it, you'd better invite us in."

Tonnie looked from John to Andrea and back again. Finally, she nodded and swung the door wide. "Might as well. But you can't stay long. I'm expecting company." She led them into the apartment where the hall opened into a wide room with a spectacular view. Walled with glass, the room overlooked Chicago's Magnificent Mile and the white dots of boats in Lake Michigan's harbor beyond. Wingate Kirkland was wealthy, all right. In real estate as well as beautiful women.

Reaching a cream chair, Tonnie sat and curled her feet under her like a cat.

She was beautiful, John had to admit. Her dark hair glowed with auburn highlights. Her model-slim body moved with grace and confidence. And her eyes were the kind that drew a man in.

But even in the same room with this dark beauty, John had a hard time keeping his eyes off Andrea. Gnawing her bottom lip, she perched on the edge of the sofa as if sheer will was the only thing keeping her from bolting.

He forced his attention back to Tonnie. "About Kirkland's gun?"

"I went to a gun show with him about a month ago. He bought several guns."

"What kinds of guns?"

"Search me. I don't know anything about the things."

"Were they hunting rifles or handguns?"

"Mostly rifles. He bought one handgun, though. A little one. He had me pick it up to see how it fit in my hand."

"Did he keep the gun here at the apartment?"

"No. He took it to Wisconsin with him. He said he bought it for her. Just like he did everything for her. Even when she didn't deserve it."

Andrea turned to him, eyes wide with shock. "He never bought me a gun. I don't even know how to shoot one. I've never shot a gun in my life."

John nodded to Andrea. He wanted to tell her it was all right. That he'd get to the bottom of it. That he'd find the truth. But it wasn't all right. And he wasn't sure he wanted to know the truth.

He pulled the rug dealer's flyer from his briefcase. "Do you know this man?"

"Hank?"

"How do you know him?"

"He was here at the apartment for a party once."

"A party? Hank Sutcliffe hauls rugs for a living. He doesn't seem the type a millionaire like Wingate Kirkland would party with."

Tonnie shrugged. Stretching her fingers out, she studied her manicure as if she had nothing better to do.

John let out a disgusted breath. Her nonchalance didn't fool him. Witnesses with something to hide often resorted to grooming gestures to cover up tension. "When was this party?"

She looked up from contemplating her nail polish. "Last week. Right before Win left for Wisconsin."

"Who else was at the party?"

"What business is that of yours?"

He ignored the comment, trying to read her body language instead. "Just the three of you?"

She shrugged. "It's Hank that's in trouble, isn't it?"

"I need to talk to him. Do you know where I can find him?"

"He's living at one of Win's apartment buildings. Just moved in."

Sutcliffe had moved into one of Kirkland's buildings? This was getting stranger by the minute. "Do you know how Kirkland became friendly with Hank Sutcliffe?''

"Yeah. He said *she* introduced them." Tonnie shot a glare at Andrea.

"I didn't. I don't know him." Andrea threw her hands out in front of herself as if warding off physical blows.

"I guess they were old friends," Tonnie kept on. "Good enough friends that Win offered him a job and a place to live down here to get him away from her."

Andrea faced John. Her wide blue eyes pleaded. Her voice ripped from her throat in a strangled whisper. "I've never met Hank Sutcliffe in my life, I swear."

John swallowed into a dry throat. The way evidence was piling up against Andrea, there wasn't a chance in hell he should believe her. But God help him, the gun, the news she knew Hank Sutcliffe— none of it changed a thing. He still wanted to believe she was telling the truth.

There weren't enough antacids on the planet to overcome the ache in his gut this time.

Chapter Six

Andrea looked up at the battered six-story building and fought back the cold tendrils of memory threatening to choke her. She knew this neighborhood well. Too well. It was a neighborhood of poverty, drugs and the tyranny of gangs. A neighborhood where the air itself pulsed with desperation and smelled of despair.

The neighborhood she'd grown up in.

The rhythm of rap music and a dribbled basketball mixed with the shouts of teens playing a game in a court between buildings. The smell of frying oil wafted from a restaurant—one of the few businesses open in the row of boarded-up buildings nearby. A gust of wind whipped down the street, its chill penetrating her bones. But the chill was nothing compared to the aching cold memories this place engendered.

Or the icy dread she'd felt while talking to Tonnie Bartell.

Every word out of the woman's mouth was an accusation. Every answer she gave to John's questions pointed back to Andrea. She tried to swallow the fear inching up her throat. It was as if she'd been plunged into an alternate universe. A universe where someone was trying to kill her with a black truck, everyone hid a dangerous secret and no matter what happened, it was her fault. Crossing her arms over her chest, she rubbed her upper arms with her hands.

"Are you cold?" John unbuttoned his overcoat.

She held up a hand. "I'm fine. Thanks."

He gave her a skeptical frown.

"At least I will be fine once we find Hank Sutcliffe and he confirms he's never met me."

John nodded as if he believed her. But why would he? Since they'd come to Chicago, they'd found nothing that suggested anyone but her had killed Wingate. Couple that with the phone call he'd gotten on his cell earlier and Tonnie's not-too-veiled suggestion that Andrea and Hank Sutcliffe were having an affair, and John would be crazy to believe her.

She walked faster toward one of the buildings. "I sure hope we can find Hank Sutcliffe. It's easier to get lost in this neighborhood than most people know. Especially if you want to."

"You sound like you have experience." He gave her a pointed look.

She tried not to turn away under his scrutiny. The fact was, she did have experience. Too much. But telling him about it wouldn't convince him she was telling the truth about Wingate's death. Quite the contrary. Telling him about her past would only convince him she'd married Wingate for his money, just as Tonnie had said.

She forced a laugh. "I have enough experience to know that many of the residents here would rather eat dirt than talk to cops. Or district attorneys."

He held up a finger. "Unless they don't know I'm a district attorney." He fished the rug flyer out of his briefcase and started for the teens playing basketball.

A couple of kids watched their approach suspiciously. When they stepped onto the court, a tall pock-marked boy with a gold cap on one front tooth stepped forward. "What do you want, cop?"

The basketball stopped bouncing. The other kids gathered behind the spokesman.

John held up his hands, palms outward. "I'm not a cop. I'm an attorney. I'm looking for this man." He held out the flyer.

"Should have known. You dress too good for a cop." The kid glanced at the picture. His eyes showed neither surprise nor recognition. "So? What he do?"

"Nothing. He inherited some money. If you direct me to him, he might give you a share for the favor."

"I'm sure he'd give me some out of the goodness of his lily-white heart. Too bad I don't know him." The kid grinned, showing off his gold tooth, and dropped the flyer. The wind caught the paper and plastered it against the chain-link fence enclosing the basketball court.

"Yeah. Too bad." John turned away from the kids and retrieved the flyer from the fence. After returning to the sidewalk, he glanced at Andrea and shrugged. "So much for that idea."

"The prospect of someone showing up and offering money is pretty foreign to people here. A fantasy, really."

"Good thing I have another idea." He walked beside her until they reached the next building. As they approached the door, a woman bustled out, a little girl in tow. John stood in their path and held out the flyer. "Excuse me. I'm an attorney looking for this man. Have you seen him?"

The woman squinted at the picture. "Don't know." Clutching the girl's hand, she pulled her around John.

John moved with them, blocking their path. "He owes a lot of money in child support."

The woman glowered. "I guess he has a lot of company."

"Have you seen him?" He offered her the flyer again.

She didn't even pretend to look at the picture this time. "I said, I don't know." She pulled the girl around John and hurried down the sidewalk.

John turned to Andrea. ''So much for compassion. Any ideas?''

Andrea nodded. She had a few. No telling if they would work, but she had nothing to lose by trying them. She took the flyer. John yanked the apartment building door open and motioned her into the lobby.

What there was of a lobby.

The odors of old cigarette smoke and rotting garbage hit her in the face with the force of a physical blow. A too-loud television set blared through walls the thickness of tissue. Sunlight struggled to shine through the grime-encrusted window over the door and failed. Not that the place would have been better for the light. At least the shadows helped hide the filthy carpet, graffiti-scrawled walls and broken light fixtures. A man with a scruffy beard and a can of malt liquor in his hand stood at the bank of scarred mailboxes.

Memories pushed into Andrea's mind, memories she'd rather let die. Shoving the memories aside, she raised her chin and approached the man. ''Sir? We're with the government, and we need your help.''

He looked her up and down before turning back to the mailboxes. He slipped a key in one and opened it.

Good thing she didn't discourage easily. Stepping toward him, she held the flyer under the man's nose. ''This man is suspected of aiding terrorists. Have you seen him?''

The man focused on the picture. "I seen him."

"Do you know where I can find him?"

He nodded. "Lives in 3C. He's home now. I just saw him before I came down for my mail."

She gave him a smile. "Thank you, sir. You're a good American."

"Damn straight." He took a swig from his can and turned back to his mailbox.

John and Andrea headed up the cement stairs. Out of the corner of her eye, Andrea spotted John's grin.

"Good story," he said. "Couldn't have thought of a better one myself."

A glow registered somewhere in the pit of her stomach at his praise. "Thanks."

They reached the third floor and opened the stairwell door. Soon they would talk to Hank Sutcliffe. Soon he would tell John he'd never seen her before. And then she could leave Sunny Vale Apartments and all the memories that went with them behind for good.

Spotting the door marked C, she pointed it out and fell in behind John.

He rapped on the door hard, the sound reverberating down the hall.

A rustle came from behind the door. The television sounds ended abruptly. Finally the knob turned, and the door inched open. A green eye peered out above the still-secured door chain. "What do you want?"

John held up his identification card. "I'm from the

district attorney's office in Dane County, Wisconsin—''

"Who sent you?"

"Can we come in?"

"Who sent you, damn it?"

Andrea stepped closer to the door. "No one sent us. We're here about my husband, Wingate Kirkland."

The man moved to close the door.

She slipped her foot between the door and the jamb, the way she'd seen John do when Tonnie had tried to slam the door in their faces. She couldn't let Sutcliffe shut them out. Not until he told John the truth. "Do you know me, Mr. Sutcliffe? Have you ever seen me before in your life?"

He leaned on the door.

Pain crushed her toes and shot up her leg. John grabbed her leg and pulled her foot out of the door. The door slammed shut. "Are you crazy? Do you want a broken foot?"

Panic tightened her throat. "He doesn't know me. He has to tell you he doesn't know me. He can't just slam the door." She pushed against John's chest until he released her. She lunged at the door, her fists cracking against wood.

"Shh." John cocked his head and held a finger to his lips.

She stopped, listening, her pulse pounding in her ears.

A faint screech penetrated the paper-thin walls. Then she heard a clatter of feet on a metal grate. She looked at John. "The fire escape?"

He nodded once. Grabbing her hand, he raced for the stairs. "Maybe we can catch him on the way down."

Heart thumping against her ribs, she ran. Her breathing echoed in her ears, drowning out the beat of their shoes on the concrete stairs. They reached the ground floor and pushed out the exit.

Cold air slapped Andrea's face and rasped in her lungs. They rounded the corner of the building. The fire escape clung to the cement block wall in front of them. Hank Sutcliffe dangled from the bottom platform. And jumped.

He hit the ground hard, falling to the concrete in a heap. Struggling to his feet, he glanced in their direction. His eyes were wide, frightened, as if they were coming after him with guns.

"Wait!" Andrea yelled.

He turned and ran, ducking around the far corner of the building.

John and Andrea raced after him. But by the time they circled the building, dark narrow alleys and junk-strewn streets were all that greeted them. Hank Sutcliffe was nowhere to be seen.

"Damn." John stopped running.

Andrea shook her head, the wind whipping her

hair against her cheeks. "He can't be gone. He can't be."

"There's no telling which alley or street he went down. Hell, he might have ducked inside one of those boarded-up buildings for all we know."

Up ahead, the thump of a car stereo shook the air and centered in the middle of her chest, stronger than her heartbeat. A rust-encrusted sedan turned the corner.

John was right. They'd never find Hank Sutcliffe now. She'd meant it when she'd said people could get lost in this place. They could get lost and never find their way out. "What do we do now?"

"We give the police this picture of Hank Sutcliffe and hope he gets picked up for something. They'll find him eventually."

His voice rang with confidence, but Andrea sensed worry creeping in around the edges. "Tell me the truth. We need him now, don't we?"

"It would be good to bring home a souvenir of our trip."

"That call you got earlier. It was about me, wasn't it?"

"In a way."

"What way?"

"The police found a gun at your house."

"A gun? The gun that shot Wingate?"

"They won't know until they find the body."

She thought of the gun Tonnie had mentioned.

"It's a small gun, isn't it? The gun Tonnie was talking about."

"Yes."

Andrea's head spun.

John grasped her elbow, steadying her. "Are you all right?"

She forced herself to straighten. "I'm fine. I just need a minute to catch my breath. I'm not used to all that running, I guess."

He dropped his hand from her arm and looked at her skeptically. "Okay. If that's all it is."

"That's all it is. Really. I just need a moment." She stepped across the sidewalk to a line of parked cars. She had to get away from John. At least for a few seconds. She'd never regain her balance with him standing so close.

Steadying herself against one of the cars, she tried to catch her breath. The thump of the electronic bass, the smell of decay, the desperation hanging in the very air closed around her throat like a strong hand. She couldn't go back to Madison and face the cops' suspicious stares and she couldn't stay here. John didn't believe her. He couldn't. Not when every time he turned around he was confronted by another lie about her.

It was just as it had been when she was a girl. Nowhere to go. No one to believe her.

The rusted-out car with the booming stereo drove slowly down the street. Kids with nothing to look forward to in life hung out the side window, staring straight at Andrea. One of the teens held something in his hand. Something that looked like a gun. Above the thumping bass, a sharp pop split the air, followed by another.

He was shooting at *her*. Adrenaline slammed into her bloodstream. She had to take cover.

They had to take cover.

She raced across the sidewalk and lunged for John. "Get down!" She grabbed John's arm and pulled him to the concrete.

Chapter Seven

John flattened his body against the cold sidewalk. His pulse pounded in his ears above the crack of gunfire. He'd never carried a gun. After all the destruction he'd seen them cause, he'd never wanted to touch one of the damn things. But he'd give anything to have one now.

He raised his head slightly, trying to see where the shots were coming from. Although the car and the kids hanging out its windows looked like typical gang issue, he knew damn well they weren't. This was no random drive-by shooting. They were after Andrea. He knew it in his bones. He also knew they weren't going to get her. Not while he had something to say about it.

He moved closer to her, trying to cover her body with his, trying to protect her. Although he'd known what the popping noise was, he hadn't reacted. Not fast enough. If it hadn't been for Andrea racing away from the cover of the parked cars in order to pull him to the sidewalk, he'd probably be dead right now.

"We have to run for it." Andrea's voice rang above the fading thump of the car's sub woofer. "They'll come back to see if they got us."

"The closest cover is those parked cars." He pointed to the cars she'd been standing next to when the shooting started. The cars she'd left to save him.

Andrea pointed to a space between buildings across the street. "We can go from there to the alley."

"What if the alley's a dead end?"

"It isn't. Trust me."

He glanced down at her.

Cheek pressed to the sidewalk, she peered up at him, her eyes sparking with fear. But not panic.

He gave her a tight smile. "I'll be right behind you."

She nodded. "On three. One."

He lifted his body off Andrea. Gathering his muscles, he prepared to jump to his feet.

"Two." Andrea tensed beneath him. She reached for his hand and gave his fingers a squeeze. "Three."

They sprang upright as one. They ran for the cars, her fingers still locked with his. Once they reached the cars, they hunkered down behind them.

John paused, afraid to breathe lest the teen gunmen hear him above the rap and zero in for the kill. If they were going to get out of this, they needed help. And they needed help now.

He groped along his side. There it was. His cell phone. Help was only a call away. Among the flying bullets, he'd forgotten the damned thing. He slipped the phone from its case, punched in 911 and held it to his ear.

Hurriedly, he told the operator what was going on and where they were.

The thump of the bass grew louder.

Andrea clutched his arm. "We have to get to the alley. Now."

Leaving the line open, he slipped the phone back into its case. He grabbed Andrea's hand. They sprang from behind the car and raced across the street.

A shot screamed over their heads.

Another dose of adrenaline jolted his already saturated bloodstream. His heart pounded against his ribs. They lunged forward, making it into the alley's shadow just as a bullet pinged off the building to the right.

They didn't slow. Footfalls echoed off the buildings to either side of them. They dodged between Dumpsters. John stepped in a slushy puddle. Liquid of undetermined origin splashed up his pant legs and soaked his socks and shoes. The cloying stench of garbage clogged his throat.

The end of the alley drew closer with each stride.

His heart thundered in his chest. No. Not his heart. The pulsing beat of music.

The car's sound system.

John flattened against the wall of the alley, pulling Andrea with him.

Alarm reflected in her eyes.

He gestured to the car ahead of them. Rust paint and a cracked windshield was visible in the glow of twilight. It had circled the block and was now cutting off their escape route. A car door slammed.

A shout and footfalls echoed off the brick behind them.

"Damn. Some of the kids must have gotten out of the car before it circled the block. They're coming from both directions."

Andrea pulled his hand. "Quick! Climb in a Dumpster."

He opened the lid of the closest Dumpster and peered inside. Even on a cool November day, the smell nearly knocked him over.

Oh hell. So much for the overcoat. And the suit. His shoes were already ruined. And Andrea's green silk and cashmere coat didn't stand a chance.

Another car door slammed and voices bounced through the alley.

He was beginning to think they didn't stand a chance either. "The Dumpsters are the only things in this damned alley. They won't have to wonder where we went for long."

"Maybe long enough for the cops to get here."

"All right. Dumpster diving it is." He locked his fingers together, his hands forming a cup. Leaning down, he positioned them to allow Andrea to use them as a step.

She slipped her foot in place. With a heave, she swung a leg over the edge and slipped down into the muck.

John heaved himself up to the edge and over. The trash was soft and slick under his feet. From the smell, he'd say they were behind a restaurant whose specialty was deep-fried cabbage with a side of rancid pork fat. And ketchup, of all things. The sticky sweet scent made him gag.

Just his luck.

He lowered the lid and slipped an arm around Andrea. He could feel her heartbeat, strong and fast. Her body trembled. He gathered her close. Wanting to shield her. Wanting to protect her.

What a laugh.

She'd been the one protecting him. From ducking away from cover to pull him to the sidewalk at the first pop of gunfire to the plan to hide in the Dumpsters, she'd kept him alive.

He only hoped his phone call to the cops would return the favor.

The clang of Dumpster lids shattered his thoughts. He pulled Andrea closer against him. They weren't out of this yet. Not by a long shot. If the kids with the guns worked their way to this Dumpster, he and Andrea would be just as dead as if they'd taken bullets in the head back on the sidewalk.

The clanging grew louder. Closer. He groped through the garbage. His hand finally connected with something heavy. The wooden leg of a chair or table. He fitted it into his palm.

Andrea watched him, the sheen of her eyes visible even in the deep shadow.

He brandished his makeshift weapon.

Voices rumbled outside the Dumpster. Tensing, John waited for the lid to lift. Where were those damn police sirens?

The lid flew open. John willed his eyes to adjust to the sunlight, willed himself to see. The black barrel of a semi-automatic pistol nosed over the steel edge.

He brought the table leg down hard. A cry of pain rang out. The kid jerked back his arm. The gun clattered against the side of the Dumpster and landed somewhere outside on the pavement.

John sprang upright, swinging the table leg.

The table leg cracked against a shoulder. Another yelp. John looked into the pock-marked face of the kid from the basketball court. His lips pulled back in pain, his gold tooth glinting in the shadow of the alley. "My arm. Damn it! The guy broke my arm."

"Where's the gun?" an adolescent voice yelled.

A siren shrieked over the pounding beat of the rap.

"Let's get the hell out of here!"

"But the gun!"

"Leave it!"

Rubber soles thumped against pavement. John lifted himself over the Dumpster's edge just in time to see three boys racing down the alley. Car doors slammed. Tires screeched.

He remembered to breathe.

Turning, he focused on Andrea. Face streaked with dirt, she held a bent metal fork in her hand as if ready to take on the world.

And from the look in her eyes, she'd damn well win.

A surge of admiration tightened his gut. Andrea Kirkland might look delicate and vulnerable, but she was tough. Tough and smart and—

Innocent.

His mind landed on the word and latched on like a pit bull.

He didn't have any proof. Hell, everything he'd learned since coming to Chicago should add to his suspicions of her, not convince him of her innocence. But whether it made sense or not, he couldn't believe she'd killed her husband. He couldn't believe she'd kill anyone. Not the woman who'd risked her own life to pull him to safety when the bullets started flying. Not the woman who willingly dove into garbage to save their necks. Not the woman who was ready to fight by his side, even if armed only with a fork. That woman wasn't a murderer. He'd stake his life on it.

He just hoped that wasn't precisely what he'd have to do.

BY THE TIME they checked into a hotel, darkness cloaked the city. Andrea pulled on the red sweater and jeans they'd picked up at a department store to replace her garbage-marinated clothes and studied herself in the steamed mirror. Her hair framed her face in damp ringlets. Her cheeks were tinged pink by the hot shower. All in all, she didn't look nearly as weak as she felt. Only her eyes gave her away. Dark circles cupping blue.

She wrapped her arms around her middle. The hot shower might have washed away the garbage smell, but it had done nothing to alleviate the chill penetrating her bones. Had someone followed John and her to Chicago? Had that someone hired those boys to kill them? Or had Hank Sutcliffe hired the boys?

Although the police's arrival had chased the boys away, the police hadn't seemed to have answers about who the kids were. They'd only had hours of questions and more than a few suspicious looks. Either they'd pegged her and John as a couple of yuppie addicts venturing into the city for a score, or they were protecting their turf from an out-of-state DA. Either way, they weren't much help.

A knock sounded on the hotel-room door. "It's John. I have dinner."

She hadn't realized how much she needed to see him until she heard the sound of his voice. Crossing the room, she peered through the peephole and into the hall, just to make sure.

Distorted by the wide-angle lens, he stood on the other side of the door, a pizza box balanced on one hand. He had showered as well and replaced his soiled suit with a rugby shirt and jeans they'd picked up along with the sweater and jeans she wore. The shirt was open at the collar, showing a tease of chest hair.

The feel of his arm wrapped around her while they'd crouched in the Dumpster echoed along her nerves. What she wouldn't give to be able to open the door right now and melt into his arms. So safe. So warm.

She shook her head, trying to banish the image, the need. The last thing she could allow herself to do was fall into his arms. As much as they'd been through in the past two days, he wasn't her savior. No matter how much she needed him to be. She had to remember that. Bracing herself, she pulled open the door.

John held up the box. "I hope you're in the mood for pizza."

The aroma of tomato sauce, mozzarella and pepperoni hit her in a wave. Her stomach growled. It felt like years since she'd eaten. "It smells great."

"Then can I come inside?"

"Of course." She stepped aside, embarrassed she'd been standing in the middle of the opening, barring him from the room.

Stepping through the narrow door, he brushed her arm. He paused, looking down at her.

A shiver worked its way over her skin at the light touch. He was so close she had only to lean forward to find that place in his arms again. She wondered if it would still feel as warm. As safe.

Swallowing hard, she forced her feet to carry her into the room. A bed dominated the space, leaving just enough space for a simple armoire that housed the television. She gestured to the lack of space. "I don't know where you want to set the pizza. The bed seems like the only place, I suppose."

He looked down at the bed and then back at her. If she wasn't mistaken, some of the heat she'd felt at his touch registered in his eyes. Pulling his gaze from her, he set the box on the multi-colored spread and flipped open the lid. Pizza steam rose in the air. "Dig in."

She stepped up to the bed, lifted a piece from the box and forced herself to take a bite. The pie was hot, the crust crispy and the cheese plentiful and elastic. But as good as she knew it must be, she could hardly taste it. The only thing she was aware of was the heat of John's gaze resting on her face.

She looked up and met his eyes. She swallowed, the bite of pizza lodging like a lump in her throat. "What?"

"I can't help wondering how you got to be so tough."

"Me?"

"You look so delicate, so vulnerable. Yet there's something inside you that's stronger than tempered steel. How did you get to be that way?"

She shook her head. He had her wrong. All wrong. "I'm not strong. I try to be, but I'm not."

The corner of his mouth quirked upward in a half smile. "Could have fooled me. Where did you learn to keep your head in the midst of flying bullets?"

She'd been scared out of her skin when she'd heard the gunshots, so scared her mind had shut down, allowing her to operate without thinking, without feeling. "I guess I've gotten used to ducking after the past few days."

"It takes longer than a few days of hardship to learn to react the way you did. I've been part of the criminal justice system for years. I've seen the aftermath of shootings. I've prosecuted the shooters. I know the sound of gunfire and what kind of damage bullets can cause. Yet it took me a few seconds to realize what was going on, let alone to act. You acted on instinct."

She set down the slice and twisted her fingers in her lap.

"And how did you know the alley we ran down wasn't a dead end?" His dark eyes looked into her, through her.

Wrapping her arms around herself, she looked down, staring at the open box. She didn't want to answer his questions, didn't want to explain the hardships that had shaped her. She wasn't ashamed of her humble beginnings. Not really. If it had been something as simple as growing up on the wrong side of the tracks, she would have answered his questions without flinching. But things weren't that simple. Her mother had seen to that. Marrying Wingate had seen to that. And now that he was dead, she knew her background would just add to the long list of things suggesting she killed her husband.

But more than that, she didn't even want to remember herself. Her helplessness. Her weakness. Her desperate need for someone to believe her, for someone to care.

So little had changed.

"Tell me, Andrea. Let me in."

She blew a defeated breath through tight lips. She didn't want to tell him, didn't want to let him in. But she couldn't help it. On some level, the battle was already over. She'd lost the moment he'd pushed her out of the path of that black truck. "I didn't grow up in Wingate's social circles."

He nodded, as if he'd surmised that.

"My father left when I was young. My mother did her best, I suppose, but there was never very much money." She shook her head. "But money was never important to me. Not then and not now. I know that's hard to believe."

"I admit at first it was."

"And now?"

"Now I'm not sure."

She supposed that was better than she could have hoped. At least he hadn't made up his mind against her the way most people had. "I didn't know how good I had it until I ran away."

"You ran away? Why?"

"My mother needed men the way some people need booze or pills. She always made sure she had one around." She tried to push a laugh from her throat, but the sound lodged and turned into a groan. "I didn't understand how dependent she was on them until one of her boyfriends came into my room one night."

John's eyes grew hard. "He molested you?"

"He tried. He was so drunk, he couldn't have molested a paper bag. But that wasn't the worst of it." She paused, not wanting to go on, not wanting to remember.

"What happened?"

"When I told my mother, she got angry. Not with

him. With me. She said I was lying. She accused me of trying to make him feel unwelcome in her home.''

''So you ran away.''

''Yes.''

''To Sunny Vale Apartments. That's how you knew that alley wasn't a dead end.''

She nodded. ''A woman let me live with her in exchange for paying a share of the rent and watching her kids while she worked.''

''And that's where you met Kirkland.''

A flush rushed up her neck and pooled in her cheeks. ''I was eighteen by then. He was nice to me. Acted interested in what I had to say. Made me feel like I mattered. That's a powerful drug to a runaway who grew up without a father.''

''And he offered you a way out of Sunny Vale.''

''I don't like to think about how weak I was. How impressed by Wingate.'' She shook her head. ''I ended up being more like my mother than I could have imagined.''

''You were a kid. You were desperate.''

''Maybe. His sister, Joyce, says I latched on to his money and didn't let go.'' She shook her head. ''She was wrong. I couldn't have cared less about the money. I wanted to feel safe. I wanted to feel loved. I wanted to feel like I mattered. And Wingate ended up giving me none of those things.''

''Why didn't you tell me the truth about your marriage when we first met?''

She shook her head and kept her eyes focused on the pizza cooling and congealing in its box. "I don't know. I guess I didn't want to see that look in your eyes."

"What look?"

"The look of suspicion. As if you know what I'm all about and it's spelled M-O-N-E-Y."

He reached out a hand. Touching the point of her chin, he tilted her face back, forcing her to meet his eyes. "Do you see that look?"

"No. I guess not. What I see is worse. Pity."

He exhaled through tense lips. "You make me feel a lot of things, Andrea. But pity isn't one of them."

She swallowed into a tight throat. She had to ask. She had to know. "What do I make you feel?"

"Surprise."

"Surprise? I surprise you?" How could she surprise him? Every time he looked at her, she could have sworn he saw right through her.

"You've surprised me since I met you. But even more than that, you make me surprise myself."

"How?"

He smoothed a damp tendril back from her cheek with his fingertips, the ghost of a touch sending goose bumps over her skin. His dark eyes drilled into her. "It's been a long time since I've believed in anything. Or anyone. Not like I believe in you. I didn't know I still had the capacity."

She let his words seep into her like rain after a

long drought. Afraid that if she thought, if she moved, they would dissipate into the air as if he'd never said them.

Trailing fingertips over her cheek, he tucked her hair behind her ear.

She turned her face into his hand, soaking in his warmth, his scent, his touch. A sigh escaped her lips. She was so tired. Tired of being afraid. Tired of trying to be strong. Tired of being alone.

He cupped the back of her neck with his hand and pulled her against his strong body.

She melted into him. Melted into his warmth and the safety of his arms. She couldn't be strong anymore. She didn't even want to. She wanted him to touch her, to kiss her, to hold her and never let her go.

The bleat of his cell phone slashed the air.

Andrea stilled. Reality flooded back, dousing the warmth.

He released her and took half a step back.

Cold air filled the space where his body had been. Chills raced up her arms.

Pulling his gaze from her, he reached for the cell phone on his belt. He punched the talk button and held the phone to his ear. "Yeah?"

He paused, listening to the voice on the other end. "What is it, Al?"

Something had happened. She could hear it in his voice. She could feel it in the air.

"Fine. We'll be there." John's voice rang hard as a steel hammer against stone. He punched the off button and met Andrea's eyes. "We have to drive back to Madison tonight. The search dogs found your husband's body."

Chapter Eight

Apprehension crept up Andrea's spine as she stepped from the car John had rented and stood at the base of the familiar cobblestone drive of Wingate Estate. The gates gaped open, the drive blocked only by a ribbon of yellow tape and two uniformed police officers. Ahead, through the skeletons of bare trees, red and blue lights from several police cars throbbed and swirled across the brick mansion and the frost-bitten gardens kneeling at its feet.

A car door slammed and John stepped to her side. His breath hung like smoke in the frigid air. "The dogs found him in the woods behind the house."

Andrea nodded. It seemed strange talking about Wingate in this way. Unbelievable that he was dead, found lying in the woods where he used to hunt. "What happens now?"

"The detectives and crime scene techs have to take photographs and collect evidence before they move him. They won't be able to do much of that until morning.'' He studied her face as if trying to gauge whether or not she could take the news.

She raised her chin, but it was an empty gesture. Back in Chicago he'd said she was tough. But she didn't feel tough now. Far from it. ''The police think I did it, don't they?''

John opened his mouth as if to deny her statement, then closed it before a word left his lips. He nodded. ''The spouse is the automatic first suspect in cases like this.''

''With Win willing his entire estate to me, I imagine I make a better suspect than most.''

''Yes.''

''When they learn what Tonnie Bartell has to say, they'll be ready to lock me up and throw away the key.''

He said nothing, his silence telling her all she needed to know.

She returned her gaze to the scene in front of them. From the look of the flashing lights and cars of varying colors, all the police in the state were gunning for her. ''What will they do with me tonight?''

''They'll probably take you to the Green Valley police station.''

''Green Valley—'' Fear closed her throat.

''The Green Valley police won't be the only ones present. I know the county detective on the case. You'll be all right.''

She swallowed hard, trying to breathe. "What then? Will they arrest me?"

"Not unless they have evidence I don't know about. More likely they'll just want to ask you some questions."

Her heart dropped. With the hole still gaping in her memory, she didn't have a chance of standing up to questions. "How do I answer? I don't remember everything that happened."

"Just tell the truth, what you remember. And it wouldn't hurt to have a lawyer present."

"Won't calling a lawyer make me look guilty? I don't have anything to hide."

"It doesn't matter. You need legal protection."

She bit her bottom lip.

She felt like running away, hiding in the cabin up north and not emerging until the police had found the real murderer. Until they focused their accusing stares and leading questions on someone else.

John ran a finger down her arm. "It's going to be okay. I'll be there for you. I'll protect you."

Warmth chased his touch, just as it had in the Chicago hotel room. It was nice thinking he'd be there for her, that she wasn't alone anymore. But she had a sinking feeling it wasn't as simple as he'd have her believe. "You can't protect me and still do your job, can you?"

"No, he can't." A heavyset man in a wrinkled brown suit ducked under the yellow crime scene tape

across the driveway and ambled toward them. The
flashing red and blue lights reflected off his balding
head, making him look like some sort of macabre
clown. "I sure as hell hope he's learned something
from his past mistakes."

John grimaced and let his hand fall to his side.
"Andrea Kirkland, this is Detective Al Mylinski."

The detective's shrewd eyes sized her up. "Mrs.
Kirkland, you will have plenty of opportunity to call
a defense attorney to protect you, if that's what you
want. I'm a heavy believer in the Constitution. John
must have forgotten that."

John gave Mylinski an apologetic nod. "I'm sure
you'll be open-minded about this case, Al. I'm just
not sure others will."

Like Police Chief Gary Putnam and the rest of the
Green Valley police department. A chill sank into
Andrea's bones. She looked toward the silhouettes
moving in the flashing lights near the house. She had
no doubt Chief Putnam was up there, looking for
evidence against her. Setting her up for a murder
charge would be just as effective as killing her, if he
or one of the other Green Valley cops wanted to keep
what she'd witnessed quiet. Once she was convicted
for murdering Wingate herself, no one would believe
what she'd seen, even if her memory returned.

"You have only to cooperate, Mrs. Kirkland, and
everything will work out fine."

Andrea swung her attention back to Detective Mylinski. She raised her chin and straightened her spine. "I'll do whatever it takes to find the truth."

The hum of an engine and a flash of headlights pulled into the mouth of the driveway. A late-model Mercedes stopped behind John's car. One of the uniformed officers approached it. Bending, he talked softly to the people in the Mercedes.

The car's passenger door flew open. "I don't care what you say. I have a right to see him." A woman's screech cut the air like a knife through tender flesh.

Andrea would recognize that voice anywhere. "Joyce." She glanced over her shoulder in time to see her sister-in-law, Joyce Pratt, crawling from the passenger seat. Her blond hair caught the headlights, its color as brassy as her voice.

Detective Mylinski stepped toward the woman and raised his hands to stop her rush up the driveway. "I'm sorry, ma'am. This is a crime scene. You can't go beyond the tape."

The woman slammed against his hands full force. She clawed at his arms, trying to push past him. "Let go of me. He's my baby brother. I have a right to see him."

"Sure you do. That's why you can visit him at the morgue tomorrow."

"The morgue. Oh God. The morgue." She slumped against the detective. A sob shook her shoulders.

The driver's door of the Mercedes opened and

Joyce's husband Melvin climbed out. A bookish-looking man whose only conversational skills seemed to be comprised of the words *yes* and *dear,* Melvin huddled behind his wife, pulling his over-sized parka tighter around his shoulders. "It's all right, dear."

"All right?" Joyce turned her tear-filled fury on her husband. "Of course it's not all right. They won't let me see Wingate. They won't even let me say goodbye."

Detective Mylinski sighed. "I'm sorry for your loss, ma'am. But you'll have to wait until tomorrow."

Joyce's head snapped around, a belittling comment obviously poised on her lips. But before she could deliver the insult, her gaze latched onto Andrea. "You."

Andrea braced herself for the tirade to come.

Joyce pointed a bony finger. "She's the one you want. She's the one who killed Wingate."

Mylinski motioned to the uniformed officer behind Joyce. "Please take Mrs.—"

"I have a right to be here. More right than that gold-digging whore. She murdered my brother."

Melvin placed a hand on her shoulder.

Joyce shoved it away. "Maybe I could have stopped her if I hadn't been in Paris. If I'd been home, maybe I could have kept her from killing dear Wingate." A sob spewed from her red-lined lips.

Mylinski grimaced and turned to the officer. "Take these fine people to the Green Valley police station. We'll want to get statements from them."

Joyce smoothed a hand over her hair. She smiled down her nose at Mylinski as if he were a servant who'd obeyed her orders. "You can bet I'll tell you the truth. Unlike some people who only know how to lie, manipulate and steal." She gave Andrea one last glare before following the officer, Melvin in her wake.

Andrea exhaled. Dealing with Joyce was always a chore. Dealing with her tonight was impossible.

"If you'll come with me, Mrs. Kirkland, I'd like to ask you a few questions." Detective Mylinski gestured to a brown sedan parked just inside the yellow tape.

Dread settled into her bones like the chill of approaching winter. She forced her feet to follow the detective. The only thing that kept her from bolting was John walking beside her.

A group of people gathered near the crime scene tape talking with the remaining officer. Andrea recognized Ruthie Banks's slight build. Her pixie face was obscured by her parka's wide hood, but nothing could hide the twist of contempt on her lips.

An older man stood next to her conversing with the officer, his arms crossed over an ample belly. Probably Ruthie's father, the judge. Although Andrea had never met him, Wingate had supported him in the last election, and she knew Judge Banks's reputation. Tough on crime. And criminals. If the police arrested her, Gerald Banks would probably love to preside over the trial. If for no other reason than to rid his neighborhood of the criminal scourge she represented.

"You killed him." A soft voice filtered through the darkness.

Shivers sprinkled Andrea's skin. She turned in the direction of the sound.

Her housekeeper, Marcella, stood behind her. She held a rosary in her work-roughened hands, the iridescent oyster-shell beads glowing red and blue with the flashing squad car lights. Eyes narrowed to brown slits, she stared at Andrea as if she were evil incarnate.

"I didn't kill him, Marcella. I swear."

Marcella shook her head as if refusing to hear her. She crossed herself. "May God forgive you, missus. Because I never will."

John stepped between her and Marcella, as if trying to block her from the woman's curse.

Mylinski opened the back door of his sedan. "Mrs. Kirkland?"

Almost grateful for the escape, Andrea ducked inside, trying not to think of Joyce's accusations, trying not to see her neighbors' glares or hear her housekeeper's soft curse. She'd felt the stares and heard the whispers since the day she'd married Wingate.

But that was nothing compared to this. Now they believed she was a murderer. A monster.

She looked up at John, catching a glimpse of him just before the detective's body moved between them, and he slammed the car door, the sound as final as a life sentence.

She wrapped her arms around herself and held on. Only a few short hours ago, she'd been warm in John's arms. Safe. But now she was alone again— more alone than she'd ever felt before. And it was worse because now she knew what she was missing.

JOHN SAT in the cubicle adjoining the interrogation room and peered through the one-way glass. Andrea huddled next to the small table, arms crossed over her chest. Chin held high, she stared at the glass with empty eyes.

John couldn't tear his gaze away. She was such a mix between beauty and fight, vulnerability and toughness. She made him want to protect her and fight by her side all at once. Anything, as long as he was near her.

"You sure you want to watch this one, Ace? Or should I call one of the other ADAs?"

He glanced up at Mylinski. The detective watched him over a steaming foam cup, no doubt waiting for him to duck out gracefully.

Although it would be the smart way to go, he couldn't take it. He'd promised Andrea he'd be there for her. And even if he couldn't do much to protect her from behind the glass, he couldn't abandon her. Not when he'd given his word. "Don't bother calling the DA's office, Al. But I will take a cup of that sludge you like to call coffee."

Mylinski shot him a dour look and went back out the door. A minute later, he returned with another foam cup and Gary Putnam on his heels.

Putnam gave John a nod so precise and snappy, it looked like a salute. "Cohen."

John returned the nod. He hoped Putnam was planning to stay in the cubicle and observe. Andrea's nerves were frayed as it was. The last thing she needed was to have one of Green Valley's finest locked in a room with her firing questions. She still believed her call to the Green Valley police station had caused the black truck to show up. And for all he knew, she was right. Hell, for all he knew, the driver of the black truck could be Putnam himself. "Have a seat, Chief."

The man gave his head a sharp shake. "I'll stand."

John looked to Mylinski to see which of them— or both—would interrogate Andrea. He held his breath.

Finally Mylinski set down his coffee. Picking up a thick file and cradling it in the crook of one beefy arm, he moved for the door.

John released the breath. A minor victory. He

peered through the glass into the room where Andrea was sitting.

Mylinski ambled into the room. He laid the file on the table beside her and pulled a piece of paper from it. "Mrs. Kirkland, I just want you to know that you have the right to remain silent. If you give up this right, anything you say can be used against you in a court of law."

Andrea sucked in a breath. "Are you arresting me?"

"No. I just want you to know your rights up front. You also have the right to an attorney. If you cannot afford one, one will be appointed by the court. Do you understand these rights?"

Andrea nodded.

Mylinski slipped a sheet of paper from the file folder and slid it toward her across the desk. "Sign it, please." He pulled a pen from his pocket and offered it to her.

Picking up the pen with shaking fingers, she signed at the bottom.

Detective Mylinski collected the pen and paper. After signing it and noting the time, he returned it to the file folder. Mylinski did things by the book, all right. John had always liked prosecuting cases the detective investigated for just that reason. Once Mylinski compiled enough evidence to levy charges, they would stick.

At the moment, that didn't seem to be such a good thing.

Mylinski dropped the thick file on the desk with a thud and narrowed his eyes on Andrea. "Andrea, you killed your husband, didn't you?"

Andrea leaned forward. "No. I didn't kill him. I swear."

"I'm sorry, Andrea. After what we found in the house and on the grounds, there really isn't any doubt you did it."

She opened her mouth to protest.

He held up a hand. "Before you say anything more, let me call Chief Putnam in here. Maybe you can explain to us what happened."

Andrea's eyes went wide.

John gripped his coffee cup, the foam creaking under his fingers. The cup broke, sloshing hot coffee over John's hand. "Damn." He shook his hand. As hot as the coffee was, what was going on behind the glass pained him more. Andrea was so frightened. So confused. He couldn't let Putnam question her. He rapped his knuckles on the glass.

Mylinski spun in the direction of the sound. Heaving a sigh, he picked up the file from the table and ambled to the door. He popped back into the cubicle, shutting the door behind him. "What's up? This had better be good."

Inside the interrogation room, Andrea dragged in a relieved breath.

John did as well. He turned and met Mylinski's gaze. "Didn't she ask for an attorney?"

"Not that I heard," Putnam said.

He ignored the chief, keeping his attention glued to Mylinski. "She should have an attorney present."

Mylinski shook his head, as if he saw right through John's smoke screen. "I Mirandized her. You heard it. That's all I'm required to do. We got to talk, Ace." He turned to Putnam. "You want to take a shot, Putnam? I'll join you in a minute."

John held up a hand. "You do the questioning. Not Putnam."

Mylinski's brows shot toward his nonexistent hairline. "Why?"

"Just do it. As a favor to me."

"No favors. Not unless you tell me why." He reached into his pocket and pulled out a piece of candy. Unwrapping the cellophane, he popped it into his mouth and waited for John's answer.

John glanced at Andrea sitting so small, so scared in the interrogation room. "She thinks someone in the Green Valley police department was driving that truck that ran her car into the quarry."

Mylinski choked on his candy. Holding up a hand, he coughed until he cleared his throat. "And why does she think that?"

John filled him in on Andrea's returning memory, her phone call to the police station and the subsequent appearance of the black truck. "I hate to say it, Putnam, but you and your officers were the only ones who knew she saw her husband's murder.''

Putnam flushed red. "I resent what you're implying. My men are good cops, honest cops."

"I don't doubt it. But..." He left his sentence hanging, the implication clear.

Putnam's flush deepened. "You son-of-a-bitch. I don't believe this."

Mylinski held up a hand. "Before we start something here, I didn't tell you what else we found in the house."

John pulled his gaze from Putnam and focused on Mylinski. "What?"

"Listening devices. The phones were tapped. So whoever tapped them would have heard that call. And whoever tapped them could've tried to run Andrea Kirkland into that quarry."

A smile curled Putnam's thin lips.

Mylinski gestured toward the interrogation room. "Go on in, Gary. I'll be right there."

Putnam looked from Mylinski to John and back again. Finally he nodded in his military-man way, picked up the file Mylinski had dropped on the chair and pushed into the interrogation room.

Andrea's eyes flared wide when she saw him.

John's gut clenched. He could feel her fear even through the glass.

Mylinski stepped in front of him, blocking his view. "To tell you the truth, I don't know if the widow Kirkland killed her husband or not. Something doesn't feel right about this whole situation, and I can see why you think that might mean she's innocent. But either way, you've got to stay away from her. Protecting her is not your job, and I'm not going to cover for you while you go off on some damn self-destructive path. Nor am I going to let you screw with my investigation. Either you start thinking with the head on top of your shoulders instead of the one in your pants, or I'm going to Harrington with this. He'll have another ADA assigned to this case faster than spit.''

John pinched the bridge of his nose between thumb and forefinger. He wanted to argue, but he couldn't. Mylinski was right. He should get another ADA assigned to the case. He should get as far away from Andrea Kirkland as humanly possible. But he couldn't. He'd told her the truth in Chicago. He believed in her as he hadn't believed in anything in a very long time. No matter what the consequences, he couldn't leave her twisting in the wind.

However, if he wanted to protect her, he had to be smart about it. He had to know when to cut his losses. And he had to stay away from her from here on out. If he didn't, not only wouldn't he be able to protect her, he wouldn't even be able to protect himself.

He leveled Mylinski with a pointed stare. "Fine,

Al. You win. I'll go home. I'll stay away from Andrea Kirkland. I'll let you do your job.''

Mylinski nodded and took a slurp of coffee to wash down his candy. "I sure as hell hope so. Because I like you too much to watch you ruin your career over a woman. Even if she might be worth it.''

Chapter Nine

Andrea leaned her elbows on the scarred table in the interrogation room and buried her face in her hands. Detective Mylinski and Chief Putnam sat on either side of her at the table questioning her. Questioning? Who was she kidding? They seemed to have made up their minds that she had killed Wingate before they stepped in the room.

She had to convince them she hadn't. She had to persuade them to listen to the truth.

"It sounds like your marriage was hell, Andy. Can I call you Andy?"

Detective Mylinski's voice had softened since he'd come back into the room. So much so that she had to keep reminding herself he wasn't her friend.

He leaned forward, concern etched on his face. "If I had a husband like that, you can bet I'd want to get away from him as fast as I could."

"Yes. That's it. I wanted to get away. Like I told you before, I was planning to leave that night."

"And then he came home unexpectedly."

"Yes."

"Here you'd planned your escape for months. You'd squirreled away money. And the SOB shows up just as you were leaving. You had to have been desperate."

"I was. At least I think I was. I don't remember." She held her hand up to her forehead. Their questions were giving her a headache.

"Did he find out you were leaving him that night? Did he try to stop you?" The detective leaned forward as if to confide an intimate secret. "Did he hit you, Andy?"

"I don't think so. I don't know."

Chief Putnam rolled his eyes, but said nothing. Detective Mylinski lowered his voice. "He threatened to hit you, didn't he? You told John that the day you first visited his office."

She looked down at the folder in Detective Mylinski's hands. So that's what was inside. John's notes from their first meeting. A pang registered in her chest. A ridiculous reaction. It was John's job to prosecute. It was his job to help the police. She couldn't expect him to keep his notes secret, as if the contents were a private tête-à-tête between lovers. "Yes. Wingate often threatened to hit me."

"You couldn't let him know what you planned to do that night," Mylinski continued. "So you found his gun. The one he bought for you."

She shook her head. ''That's not the way it happened.''

''No one blames you for killing the bastard, Andy.
You had no choice. Not if you wanted to save your
own skin. Anyone would understand that.''

''No. It didn't happen that way.''

''How did it happen?''

''I don't— I don't remember.''

''Sometimes we block awful things from our
minds. Awful things that we've done. Is that what
happened, Andy? Because you don't have to feel
guilty. Anyone could see you had no choice in what
you did. Anyone would have done the same thing in
your place.''

''I didn't kill him. I just don't remember what happened.''

Mylinski leaned forward. The overhead lights reflected off his balding pate, crowning his head like a
halo. ''What do you remember, Andy?'' His voice
was low. Gentle. As if he'd run out of speculation.
As if he was finally ready to listen.

She took a deep breath and closed her eyes, trying
to see the memories in her mind as if they were playing out on a movie screen. ''I heard a shot. I saw
him fall to the floor. His eyes were open, staring. He
made a sound, a gurgle low in his throat. There was
blood. So much blood. It soaked into the Persian
rug.''

"That's why you had to get rid of the rug, wasn't it, Andrea?" Chief Putnam snapped.

Startling at the sharpness in his voice, she opened her eyes. "I didn't—"

"That's why you rolled his body in the rug."

"No, I—"

"And you had help, didn't you, Andrea? Someone helped you bury the rug with Kirkland inside. Someone helped you replace it with a new rug. Did that someone help you shoot your husband as well?"

"Hank Sutcliffe." The name blurted from her lips. The name of a man to whom she was somehow linked. A man she didn't know.

Detective Mylinski's eyebrows arched in obvious surprise. "Hank Sutcliffe helped you kill your husband?"

She shook her head. "No. I didn't kill Wingate. Hank Sutcliffe replaced the rug. Maybe he did it. Maybe Sutcliffe killed Wingate."

Putnam leveled a glower in her direction. "Who is Hank Sutcliffe, Andrea? Is he your boyfriend?"

She tightened her fists under the table. "I don't know him." She never should have mentioned Hank Sutcliffe's name. How could she explain who he was when she didn't know herself?

"Did he put you up to it, Andy?" Mylinski prodded. "Was he pressuring you? Did Hank Sutcliffe convince you to kill your husband?"

"I didn't—"

"How can you say that?" Putnam barked. "You don't remember. You said so yourself. You don't remember anything but the shot and the blood."

She looked down at the table. Her pulse pounded in her ears.

Detective Mylinski laid a hand on her shoulder. His touch was calming, soothing, entreating her to trust him, to open up. Just as his voice had been before Putnam had pounced. "You had every reason to shoot your husband, Andy. And if you were forced into it by Hank Sutcliffe, you have double the reason. I understand what happened. The judge will understand, too."

What could she say? She didn't remember. And although she knew in her heart she could never have killed Wingate, how could she possibly convince anyone else?

A knock sounded on the door.

Mylinski closed his eyes and blew out a frustrated breath. "What?"

A sheriff's deputy pushed the door wide and held it open. A short balding man with the face of a bull-dog stepped inside. Decked out in an immaculate double-breasted suit, he crossed to Andrea's chair and set his briefcase on the table in front of her. "I'm Mrs. Kirkland's attorney. You aren't questioning her without counsel present, are you, detective?"

Mylinski groaned and crooked a questioning brow at Andrea. "Your attorney?"

She glanced from the detective to the attorney and back again. She'd never seen the man before in her life.

"I'd like to speak to my client. In private."

"Fine." The detective motioned to Putnam and moved toward the door, the skeptical glower still on his face. "For the record, she never asked to speak with an attorney. If you don't believe us, you can check the video tape." He gestured to the corner of the room where a video camera hung from the ceiling recording everything. Mylinski and Putnam stepped out and closed the door behind them.

The bulldog in the expensive suit lowered himself into the chair vacated by the detective. He spread his briefcase open on the table.

Andrea watched him, unsure what to think about this new wrinkle. "I never called an attorney. Who are you?"

He stuck out a hand. "Lee Runyon. I was retained to represent you. I got here as quickly as I could."

"Retained? By whom?"

"That doesn't matter. What's important is that the police have no right to hold you here. Not unless you've done something stupid like confess."

"No. Of course not. I didn't kill my husband."

"Then let's get you out of here."

She couldn't wait to step out of this emotional torture chamber. But she wasn't going anywhere with this guy. Not until she knew more. "Who called you?"

"It doesn't matter," he repeated.

"It does matter. I have to know."

He smiled at her, his face muscles stretching stiffly as if the expression was a foreign one. "Let's just say it was someone who shouldn't have. Someone who should be more interested in prosecuting you than saving you from Detective Mylinski's formidable interrogation techniques."

A warm flush coursed through her. "It was John, wasn't it? John Cohen."

Runyon merely shrugged, but his silence was as good as a yes.

John had called the attorney. John was watching out for her. What she'd felt in that hotel room, in his words, in his touch—it was real.

Lee Runyon cocked his head, his jowls jiggling with the movement. "So are you ready to get out of here?"

Andrea nodded. She certainly was. And she couldn't wait one more second.

She had someone she wanted to thank.

JOHN LEANED BACK in the recliner and tried to get comfortable for the hundredth time in as many minutes. Opening his eyes, he looked around the room. The bright sun of mid morning peeked around the edges of the closed blinds, bars of light falling on the old wall clock across the room as it ticked off the minutes. He watched the hands click around the face, keeping his eye on all the minutes of sleep he wasn't getting.

Sleep he wasn't getting because he couldn't stop thinking of Andrea Kirkland.

He'd told Mylinski he'd stay away from her, that he'd let the detective do his job. And he had. Sort of. John doubted Mylinski would see his calling Runyon as staying away though.

He ran a hand over his face. Kicking down the chair's footrest, he sat up. Now that Runyon was fighting on Andrea's behalf, he needed to forget her and do his job. But the only way he could do that was if he dug that bottle of Jack Daniels out of the kitchen cupboard and downed the whole damn thing. Who was he kidding? One pint wouldn't be enough to forget Andrea. He'd have to go for two.

Before he could work up the ambition to heave himself from the chair, the ancient doorbell echoed through the house—Westminster chimes so out of tune the melody was hard to recognize. Just what he needed. He pushed to his feet and strode for the door. He'd buy a canister of Boy Scout popcorn or a half dozen boxes of thin mints and send the interloper on his or her way. He didn't have patience for this. Not today.

He saw Andrea through a window before he reached for the knob. Dark circles marred the tender skin under her eyes. Tension tightened the soft plumpness of her lips. She pulled her coat tight around her. Even exhausted from the long night at the police station, she was the most beautiful sight he'd ever seen.

A weight settled on his shoulders like an oxen's yoke. John wouldn't put it past Mylinski to have a tail on her. And once the detective found out she was here, John would hardly have enough time to duck before the repercussions hit the fan.

She hadn't seen him through the window. He should pretend he wasn't home. He should stay away from her as he'd promised Mylinski. But he couldn't leave her standing on his porch. He reached for the knob and pulled the door open.

She looked up at him, her eyes clear blue despite her fatigue. "John."

He gestured into the house. "Come in."

She stepped inside. Her gaze roamed around the room, taking in the plain white walls, the sparse furniture. The typical bachelor pad. He'd never really looked at his house before, the depressing emptiness of it. He saw it now as if through her eyes. Whoever said men were simply bears with furniture must have been talking about him.

She turned back to him. Her eyes searched his. "If this is a bad time, I'll go."

Bad time? It was the worst possible time. "Stay."

"I had to see you. I had to thank you."

"Runyon did his job?"

She nodded. "He got me out of there, if that's what you mean."

"He's a son-of-a-bitch, but he's the type of son-of-a-bitch you want to have on your side."

"You shouldn't have called him." She stepped toward him. Even after a stress-filled night at the police station, she still smelled of the hotel's herbal shampoo and the sweet scent of woman.

He breathed in deeply. "I couldn't leave you in that interrogation room. No innocent person should have to go through that."

She looked down at the floor and shuddered, as if reliving the interrogation. "Detective Mylinski thinks I killed Wingate. At least that's what he kept saying. And Chief Putnam— Every time he asked me a question, I kept seeing that black truck."

The bombshell Mylinski had dropped on him at the police station echoed in John's memory. "Putnam probably had nothing to do with that truck. Your phones were tapped."

Her eyes flew wide. "What?"

"Someone tapped your phones. So the Green Valley police weren't the only ones who knew your memory started coming back that night. Whoever was listening to your calls knew, too." He reached out and touched her arm. So warm. So soft.

"Who would have tapped our phone?"

"I was hoping you could tell me."

"I don't know. Though I wouldn't put it past Wingate to be involved in things he shouldn't be."

"Criminal activity?"

"Maybe."

John's gut tightened. "You need to hire a bodyguard."

"A bodyguard?" She scrunched up her face, as if the word tasted bad on her tongue.

He'd known she wouldn't like the idea. But it didn't matter. Until he knew who wanted her dead, he was damn well going to be sure she was safe.

And he couldn't protect her himself.

He grabbed his cordless phone and glanced around the kitchen for the phone book. "I'll call Runyon and get him on it."

Andrea's hand closed around his. She slipped the phone from his hand. "Why are you doing all this, John?"

His throat tightened. What could he tell her? That he was doing it because he believed her? That he was doing it because he cared? "You deserve justice. You deserve someone to fight on your behalf."

"But why you? You're supposed to be helping the police. You're supposed to be prosecuting me, not coming to my rescue."

She had it right there. As if he needed the reminder. But it didn't matter. Somehow nothing mattered but her. "In Chicago I told you I believed in you. Well, that's not all. I care about you, Andrea. I care what happens to you.''

Tears pooled in her eyes, turning them a watery blue.

He tried to shrug, as if his admission didn't carry the weight she seemed to think it did, but the tension bearing down on his shoulders prevented them from moving.

''No one has ever stuck by me like you have. Not in my entire life.'' Andrea leaned toward him. Her gaze held his. Her lips parted.

Heat rushed through him. Want. Need. He circled her with his arms, pulling her close. Dipping his head, he claimed her mouth with his. Her lips were soft, just as he'd known they'd be. Soft and warm and intoxicating.

When he'd told Mylinski he would stay away from her, that he wouldn't help her any more, he'd assumed he had a choice. But looking into her eyes, feeling her warmth, tasting her lips, he realized how wrong he was. He had no choice.

Maybe he never did.

A HALF HOUR LATER, Andrea watched John over her ham sandwich. He'd insisted on feeding her again, but her stomach wasn't having any more luck accepting food today than it had last night. And for all his talk about the importance of eating to keep up strength, John hadn't touched his food either.

She looked out the window, trying to keep her mind off their kiss, but it was no use. She could still feel the press of his lips on hers, still taste the flavor of him. She'd never felt so warm, so safe, so at peace as she did in his arms.

And that's what scared her.

It didn't take much to draw parallels between the need she felt for John and the need that had led her mother to choose a man over her own daughter—the same need that had convinced Andrea to marry Wingate Kirkland.

She was lucky that kiss hadn't gone further. John would only have had to crook his finger and she would have followed him to his bedroom. Even now the desire to kiss him again, to make love with him haunted her.

John looked up at her. Sighing, he set down his fork. "You're about as hungry as I am, aren't you?"

She forced a smile to her lips. "Less."

"I keep going over the conversation I had with Al Mylinski at the police station. He's not convinced you killed your husband."

"He could have fooled me. He seemed to already have me tried and convicted."

John shook his head. "Not Mylinski. He's not one to narrow an investigation down to one suspect prematurely. Not until the evidence is in. He's very thorough."

"Maybe the evidence is in."

"No. If he had enough evidence, he would have arrested you."

"So what are you saying?"

"If we can come up with something, anything that points to the person who really killed Kirkland, I'm sure Mylinski will look into it."

Andrea nodded. "So how do we go about doing that?"

"We figure out who has as much to gain from your husband's death as you do. And then we find a way to prove it."

"Whoever it is didn't kill Wingate for his money. I'm his only beneficiary."

"What if something happens to you?"

A shiver crept up her spine. The image of the black truck surfaced in her mind along with the crack of gunfire. "Something like being hit by a truck or a stray bullet?"

John nodded. "Or being convicted of murder. If any of those things happened, who would inherit?"

"I suppose Joyce would."

John nodded. "Then we start with Joyce."

Chapter Ten

Joyce's husband, Melvin, had always struck Andrea as meek at best. But today, standing spread-legged in front of the door to block her and John from entering his house, he seemed anything but. "No, you can't speak to her. Joyce has dealt with enough. I won't let you put her through any more."

John nodded, his face a mask of perfect understanding. "I know this is hard on her. But I need her help."

"She's helped enough. She sat in the police station all night. She's finally sleeping. I'm not going to wake her up and let you put her through all that again."

"I'm sure she'll want to help, Melvin." Andrea tried to make her voice as calm and understanding as John's had been.

Melvin narrowed his eyes. "Why are you here? Joyce says you killed Wingate. She's not going to be happy to see you."

John held up a hand. "I asked Andrea to come. There are some inconsistencies between Andrea's version of events and Joyce's. I think we should find out if these inconsistencies point to another murderer altogether."

Andrea gave her brother-in-law her best smile. "What do you say, Melvin? May we come in?"

Melvin's eye twitched, a tick that showed itself whenever he was under stress, which seemed to be whenever Andrea saw the poor guy. "Absolutely not. I won't stand—"

"Stand aside, Melvin." Joyce's shrill voice shattered the quiet blanketing the upscale suburban neighborhood. "I'm not afraid of that little gold digger. And if the man wants to examine inconsistencies, or whatever his line of bull is, I'm more than happy to oblige."

Melvin shrank back into the house.

John stood to the side and allowed Andrea to squeeze past him and through the door. She caught the essence of cinnamon, musk and male, the scent bringing back the feel of his embrace this morning. The taste of his kiss. A tremor fluttered in the vicinity of her stomach. What she wouldn't give to stop in her tracks, to lean against him, to soak up his strength instead of standing on her own.

She couldn't do that. Besides, if she didn't find some evidence that someone besides her killed Wingate, she wouldn't have to worry about standing on

her own. She'd be spending the rest of her days behind bars.

She forced her feet to move past him and into an
entry hall the size of a small ballroom. Looking up
to the sweeping staircase, she met the daggers in
Joyce's gaze.

Her sister-in-law descended the staircase and
shifted her attention to John. "Now what lies of hers
did you want me to refute?"

Andrea pressed her lips into a tense smile. After
six years as Wingate's wife, she should be immune
to Joyce's venom. She wasn't.

John focused on Joyce. "You mentioned you just
returned from Paris. What day was that?"

She narrowed her eyes. "Wednesday."

"You're sure about that?"

"Of course. I keep telling myself if I'd only come
home Monday as I'd originally planned, maybe I
could have prevented what happened to Wingate."

"And how would you have done that?"

"I visit my brother often. If I had been at the estate, she couldn't have killed him. I would have
stopped her." She turned a glare on Andrea.

"How do you know when your brother was
killed?"

Joyce's gaze snapped back to John. "I—I guess I
don't."

"Then how do you know that you could have prevented his death if you had come home two days earlier?''

She glanced around the room, seemingly at a loss to explain.

''Do you have your plane ticket handy?''

''Why? You want to check the date? You can believe me. It *was* Wednesday.''

John wrinkled his brow. ''Well, I'm afraid that doesn't make sense. At Wingate Estate last night, you said you'd voted for Dex Harrington. I believe you said you went into the voting booth and marked your ballot for him. The election was Tuesday. How did you go into the voting booth and mark your ballot for him if you were still in Paris?''

''I—'' Joyce looked around the room.

''She filled in an absentee ballot, Mr. Cohen. You have heard of those?'' Melvin narrowed his already beady eyes and stepped up behind his wife.

''I've never heard of them being marked while in a voting booth, Mr. Pratt.''

''It's merely an expression. Nothing more.''

''Really?''

''Really. I picked up Joyce at the airport. I saw her get off the plane. She returned home last Wednesday.''

John held up his hands, as if surrendering. ''Not a problem. I'm sure the airline records and the voter registration rolls will back up your story. A couple of subpoenas should answer any questions.''

Melvin's hands balled into fists by his sides. "Even if voter registration shows Joyce was in town last Tuesday, it proves nothing."

"Maybe not. But it is an inconsistency I'm sure the police will be interested in following up."

Hands on her hips, Joyce stared down at them from where she'd stopped on the third step. "You tell the police they shouldn't be spending their time on ridiculous things like that. They should be putting her behind bars." Joyce swung her attention to Andrea, her lips pulling back from her straight, white teeth in a snarl. "You're in more trouble than you know."

Andrea forced herself to meet Joyce's stare. "Is that a threat, Joyce?"

"Not a threat. A promise. You never should have killed Wingate. Now you're done for. Your life of luxury is over. Now your gravy train has run out."

John glanced from Andrea to Joyce. "How is that so? I was under the impression Kirkland left his entire estate to Andrea."

A smile curled Joyce's lips. "Maybe he did, but she isn't going to be able to touch it. The police have frozen Win's assets. Did you know that? I heard it while I was at the police station."

Andrea raised her chin. "I've never cared about Wingate's assets, Joyce. Why should I start caring now?"

"Why? Because lawyers cost money. A lot of it."

Realization ripped through Andrea like a bullet. Joyce was right. For once in her life, she really *did* need Wingate's money. Without it, she'd have no lawyer. And without a lawyer, she'd have no defense. She turned to John. "Is it true? Can they freeze Win's assets so I can't pay for my defense?"

"It doesn't matter," Joyce snapped. She circled her arm in Melvin's. "I talked to my lawyer this morning, too. No matter what the police do, we're contesting the will. My lawyers won't let you spend a dime of that money until the court can decide who it really belongs to. Unless Win stashed away some money no one knows anything about, you've finally reached the end of your little game."

ANDREA GATHERED her coat tightly around her neck and struggled to keep her steps even as she and John escaped from Joyce and Melvin's house. She couldn't stop shivering. Moisture hung in the air, penetrating her coat. The wind held the scent of snow on the way. But nothing could match the chill of Joyce's accusations that she wanted Wingate's money. Nothing could match it, because after all these years, her accusations were finally true.

Although she'd stashed some money away to start a new life, it wasn't nearly enough to pay for a murder defense. She didn't have to know a lot about the legal system to know that good lawyers cost good money. A lot of it. Only Wingate's fortune could finance the kind of defense she needed.

The irony lodged like a lump in her throat. She'd always told people she didn't want Wingate's money. But now…now she'd be forced to fight for it. Either that or she'd have to rely on an overworked public defender. And with the way evidence seemed to be stacking up against her, that would probably mean she could kiss her freedom goodbye.

Unless Win stashed away some money no one knows anything about… Joyce's comment rang in Andrea's ears. Her head pounded. She held her hand to her forehead.

"Are you all right?" John touched her shoulder.

What she wouldn't give to lean against him, to let his warmth wrap around her, to let his caring wipe the bitter memories away.

Memories.

She closed her eyes tight. Shadowy images played across her mind. Wingate in his study. Wingate arguing. Wingate standing near the wall behind his desk. Wingate closing…

"A safe. Wingate has a safe in the house."

"Where?"

"It's in his study. He was closing it that night. I walked in on him after dinner."

John grabbed her arms and turned her to face him. "What else do you remember?"

Her head felt as though it would split apart. Leafless trees swam in her vision. She gritted her teeth. "The safe, it's in the wall."

"Was anyone else there? Did you see anyone else?"

She tried to open her mind wider. Sweat broke out on the back of her neck. Her head throbbed. Nausea swirled in her stomach, almost doubling her over. She leaned against John, his solidness, his warmth. Gradually the headache faded, the memory dimming along with it. "It's no use. I can't remember."

John waved a hand. "It's not important." His words fell flat.

A hollow ache settled into Andrea's chest. He was trying to make her feel better. He might as well not have wasted the words. It *was* important. To her. And also to John. Vitally important. But try as she might, she couldn't cut through the fog. She couldn't see what had happened that night. "I'm sorry."

"Don't be. We have more to go on now than we had just a few minutes ago." He opened the passenger door of his car and supported her as she ducked inside. Once she'd settled into the seat and strapped on her belt, he gave her a determined smile. "Let's go find that safe."

IF BUILDINGS could talk, John had no doubt the old mansion that was the heart of Wingate Estate would sound as pompous and self-important as it looked. It was certainly a grand old house. From the crystal chandeliers and marble floors of the ballroom-sized foyer to the three-story window overlooking rolling hills to the enormous garage, the place oozed money and classic luxury. But instead of the gleaming show-place it was meant to be, the place looked a bit dirty around the edges. The after effects of two days of crime scene technicians and police dusting the place with fingerprint powder and combing every inch of the twelve-thousand-square-foot mansion.

John turned to Andrea. He could only imagine what she was feeling. Even her home resembled the wreckage her life had become. "I'm sorry about the mess. The police are pretty careful, but things still…"

She dismissed his concerns with a wave of her hand. "No need to apologize. The house was Win-gate's. Not mine."

The house wasn't hers, the apartment in Chicago wasn't hers. "Was there anything in your life that *was* yours?"

One corner of her lips curled into a half smile. "There's a cabin up north. Wingate only used it once in a while during hunting season, so I fixed it up the way I wanted it. It's small by Kirkland standards, but it's cozy. The only place that ever felt like home."

He nodded. At least she had someplace, some-thing. At least her life wasn't as desolate as his.

At least, as his had been until he met her.

Memories of the taste of her lips, the softness of

her skin, the scent of her hair niggled at the back of his mind. He wanted to pull her into his life for good, to let her make a difference in his life—permanently.

He blew a stream of air through tight lips. Too bad things didn't work that way. He of all people should know that. As soon as he started to expect too much, to want too much, he was disappointed. Betrayed.

The only sure thing in life besides death and taxes.

Andrea stopped in front of a pair of rich cherry pocket doors. "This is it. Wingate's study." Careful not to get her hands in the black powder dusting the door's handles, she slid back one of the doors.

If the rest of the place looked disordered by the police's and crime scene unit's presence, this room was a war zone. Furniture scattered the periphery, books tipped on shelves and lay in piles and black fingerprint powder coated everything from door knobs to desk. The bare hardwood floor lay exposed where the rug had once been. Several planks had actually been removed, leaving a gaping wound.

And in the center of the mess stood the housekeeper, Marcella Hernandez.

"Marcella," Andrea said.

Kirkland's housekeeper gasped in a breath and whirled around. "*Dios mio.* Missus, what are you doing here?" Crow's feet fanned out from narrowed eyes. The gentle lines of her face deepened in a frown.

John leveled an all-business stare at the woman. "We could ask you the same question, Marcella."

"I am cleaning up. Those police, they left a mess." She gestured to the disarray as if they might not have noticed.

The scene had just been released by the police, and already she was here to clean up? Either she was the most efficient housekeeper in the state, or she was here for a different reason.

"Why are *you* here?" Marcella asked anxiously.

"I'm the district attorney in charge of the investigation into Wingate Kirkland's death."

Marcella looked from him to Andrea, as if she suspected he was in charge of something that had nothing to do with the case. As if she'd been looking in his windows when he'd kissed Andrea this morning.

He stepped toward Marcella, looming over the diminutive woman. "We're looking for evidence the police may have missed."

"They missed nothing," she said, scowling at the mess in the room. "They even ripped up Mr. Wingate's floor."

Marcella seemed more broken up about the state of the house than Andrea did. Kirkland must have paid well to inspire that kind of dedication. "I'm sorry about the mess. But you'll have to wait to clean until after we are done here."

"We? Why is she not in jail?"

John flinched inwardly. Even the housekeeper had arrested, tried and convicted Andrea.

Andrea raised her chin. As petite as she was, she was taller than the housekeeper. "I didn't kill Wingate, Marcella."

The housekeeper folded her arms and glared back. "You can tell him all you want, but I know. You were never good enough for Mr. Wingate. You never loved him."

Andrea said nothing, as if she couldn't refute the charge.

Some measure of satisfaction seeped into John's bloodstream. He gave himself a mental shake. What did it matter if Andrea had never loved her husband? It had nothing to do with him. He liked Andrea. He even wanted her. Wanted her with every fiber of his body. And he knew she liked him, wanted him. But love? He couldn't even contemplate love. He would never let himself expect that much.

"She shouldn't be here. I'm calling the police." Marcella stormed out of the room.

Andrea looked to John. "What will they do if they find me here?"

"Nothing. It's your house, not the housekeeper's. You have a right to be here." Unease jabbed his gut. She might have the right to be here, but he doubted the powers that be would think *he* had the right— not to be here with Andrea at any rate.

He glanced at his watch. The last thing he needed

was for this to get back to the DA. The only thing that would come out of that was to have Wingate Kirkland's murder shifted to another assistant district attorney. One who would prosecute Andrea with everything he or she could muster. Not a good development. The only *good* development would be to find the safe and get out of this damn house. Before the police arrived.

He closed the door and locked it. Turning around, he surveyed the study. "Where do you remember seeing the safe?"

"It was in the wall."

He scanned the cherry paneling and built-in bookcases that rimmed the room. "Which wall?" He ran his hands over the cherry paneling, pressing his fingertips against each seam.

"No, it was over here, near the map." Andrea motioned to a spot next to a giant framed map of one of Kirkland's newest subdivisions on the outskirts of Madison.

John moved beside Andrea. They worked quickly, pressing each board, each seam. Finally John felt something move under his fingers. "Got it." He pressed again and the board opened on a hinge. A small safe nestled in the wall. A large dial and latch covered its front.

Andrea eyed the dial. "How do we get it open? I don't know the combination."

"Often people use a number they can remember easily. What dates or numbers were important to Kirkland?"

She thought for a moment. "Try nine, nineteen, fifty. Wingate's birthday."

He dialed in the numbers and tried the latch. It didn't budge. "Can you think of another one?"

A crease formed between her eyebrows. "How about four, fifteen, eighty?"

He began dialing the number. "What's that date?"

"The date he made his first million. At least that's the date he claimed his first million on his tax forms."

He tried the latch. No luck. "How about your birthday or your anniversary?"

She shook her head. "He never remembered my birthday or our anniversary. Every year the only present I could count on was some token sent by his secretary. She even signed his name for him."

What a piece of work. The more he learned about Kirkland, the more relieved he was that Andrea had never loved the man. "Is there any other number you can think of?"

Her eyes brightened. "Try ten, nineteen, forty-five."

"What's that date?"

She looked at the door of the study. Satisfied no one could hear her, she turned back to John. "Marcella's birthday. I used to be in charge of getting her a present every year.''

His fingers stilled. "Marcella? Why would he use the housekeeper's birthday?"

Andrea shrugged. "She's been around longer than I have. Wingate treated her more like a family member than an employee."

It was worth a shot. He dialed in the number and gave the latch a tug. The safe popped open.

Lined in blue velvet, the inside of the safe was unmarred. Empty.

"The police must have found the safe," Andrea said, her voice flat. "They must have taken whatever was in it."

"Or whoever shot your husband cleaned it out."

Andrea looked at him. "That's it then, isn't it?"

He shook his head, though inside he felt about as optimistic as she was. "That's not it. We'll figure out something."

Her eyes glistened, but she didn't allow a single tear to fall. She nodded and turned back to the safe. She looked inside once again, as if unwilling to give up the possibility of the answers to her problems being inside. Suddenly her back stiffened. "The back is off-kilter. Look."

"Sure enough." The back of the safe wasn't quite square. Reaching inside, he pried at a corner with his fingers. It was loose all right. A false back.

He pried harder. The velvet popped out. He peered into the hidden compartment. Inside were two video-tapes. ''Well I'll be damned.''

Andrea craned her neck.

He lifted the tapes out of the safe, careful to touch only the corners with his fingertips. ''Videotapes. Eight millimeter. The kind used in a small camcor-der.''

Her heart sank. ''No money?''

''Depending on what is on this tape, it could be worth far more to you than money.'' He gathered them up, put them in the pocket of his overcoat and put the safe back the way they'd found it. He wanted to slip them into a camcorder or deck right now. But that wasn't possible. Not with the police on their way. He glanced at his watch. ''Let's get out of here.''

Andrea nodded, as if she was as eager to leave as he was. She strode out of the study and led the way to the foyer, John right behind her.

Just as she reached for the brass doorknob, she froze.

John tensed. ''What is it?''

She gestured through one of the long sidelights flanking the double oak door.

He peered outside. Snow had begun to fall since they'd arrived at the house. It cascaded and swirled in the yard lights like blowing confetti, masking the darkness beyond. He squinted, trying to see past the snow to where a shadow hulked in the driveway.

A black shadow with gleaming chrome.

He sucked in a breath. "The black truck."

Chapter Eleven

Panic pounded in Andrea's head. She stared at the black hulk outside in the snow. Watching. Waiting.

A truck door slammed.

Andrea gasped. Even with the doors locked, the old house wouldn't be hard to break into. And if the driver had a gun—

John grabbed her arm and pulled her toward the back of the house. "Back door. Quick."

"Marcella." Andrea struggled against his grip. "We can't leave Marcella here."

He released her, his eyes on the door. "Find her."

She looked around the foyer, her gaze landing on the top of the staircase. "Marcella!" she called as loudly as she dared.

Silence answered her.

The house was so big, Marcella could easily be too far away to hear Andrea's shout. "We have to search for her. We can't leave her here. Not with *him* outside."

John looked back to the sidelight next to the front door. "Maybe she left. Do you see her car out there?"

Andrea joined him at the sidelight. Cupping her hand to the glass, she strained to see through the swirling snow. "I only see your car and the truck."

"I didn't see her car when we arrived. Would she have parked in the garage?"

"Maybe." She started for the garage, John on her heels. Reaching the door, she pulled it open.

Two of the garage's six bays were empty—the spot where she parked her Lexus and the space reserved for Wingate's SUV, which was still at the body shop after a fender bender. The other slots were filled with three of Wingate's late-model sports cars, and the farthest from the door housed one of his smaller sailboats.

John stepped up behind her. "She must have left."

Andrea breathed a sigh of relief. The heat of his body calmed her nerves, at least a little bit.

A thump came from the second floor.

Her relief died. "He's inside."

"Can we take one of these cars?"

"We'll have to drive right past the truck. If he has anybody with him, they'll see us." Her mind flew. She landed on the answer. "I have a better idea. Follow me."

"I'm right behind you."

She ran for the door leading to the basement. She

yanked the door open and started down the spiral staircase. John followed, pulling the door closed behind them.

They raced down the winding steps, their breathing echoing against stone walls. Halfway down the dimly lit stairs, John stumbled and fell to his knees, clutching the handrail. He was up in one stride, running behind Andrea once again.

Reaching the basement, Andrea stepped into the game room. The room ran the length of the house and was furnished with pool tables, dart boards and a full-sized bowling alley. Deer heads lined the walls.

John whistled softly. ''It's a Wisconsin sportsman's dream.''

''It was Wingate's sanctuary.'' She suppressed a shiver. Even with him dead, she felt strange entering it. As if he might pop out from behind a pool table or the old oak bar and scold her for trespassing.

Another thump rang from above. This time it came from the first floor. An unmistakable smell drifted down the stairwell.

Andrea's stomach turned. There was only one reason for that smell. ''It's gasoline. He's setting the house on fire.''

''I hope to hell there's a way out down here.'' John's voice echoed behind her.

She nodded, dodging pool tables and bar stools. ''When Wingate bought the estate, he restored the original cellar, complete with underground tunnel.''

"Convenient. How far?"

"Not far. This way." Andrea took a sharp turn near the hot tub room. Running now, she reached the tunnel door. Jerking it open, she flicked on the lights.

A mighty whoosh exploded above.

She grabbed the damp stone wall and struggled to breathe as the air was sucked from the tunnel.

John grabbed her waist from behind. He heaved her farther into the tunnel and slammed the door behind them. "Are you all right?"

She nodded, unsure her voice would carry above the beating of her heart.

"Then let's get the hell out of here."

Clinging to his hand, she forged ahead. Several more steps down, and concrete sloped under their feet. Stone banked walls and arched into a ceiling. They wound through the dim tunnel, their footsteps echoing above the roar behind them.

The lights along the tunnel walls flickered then died, casting them into blackness. Andrea broke into a sweat, whether from physical exertion or the fire above, she didn't know. The scent of smoke clogged in the back of her throat.

Finally they reached the place where the tunnel opened into the old carriage house positioned in the side of the hill. "This is it." Groping the wall, she found the light switch and flicked it on.

Nothing happened.

"The fire must have taken out the electricity." She

groped along the wall until she found shelves. Her hand closed over the cool steel barrel of a Maglite. She turned it on and directed the beam over the contents of the carriage house.

Tarps covering a line of hulking shapes filled the room. And under each tarp, four tires met the concrete floor.

John scanned the room. "Another garage."

"Wingate's collection. His pride and joy."

John walked past her. Moving from car to car, he lifted the tarps and let them fall. "A classic Bugatti. A Delorian. These cars are in mint condition. They must be worth a fortune."

"Pick one."

John raked a hand through his hair. Despite the heat licking at the backs of their necks, his eyes lit up like a little boy's at Christmas. "Let's try the fifty-seven 'Vette. I've always liked American." He tore the tarp off the red convertible.

Andrea directed the beam to the board on the wall. Each key had a hook, and each hook had a label. She grabbed the Corvette's key. She hit the automatic garage door opener. Nothing. "The electricity."

"No problem." John circled the car. He unhooked the garage door from the mechanism and raised it manually.

They wasted no time climbing into the car. John slipped the key into the ignition and the Corvette started without a hiccup. They backed out of the carriage house. Smoke and snow swirled in the car's beams. Taking the back drive, they wound over hills until they reached the main road just a mile down from the estate's driveway.

Bracing herself, Andrea looked up to the hill's crest. The proud old house stood alone in the swirling snow, flames licking from its windows and lighting up the sky.

STANDING AT HIS kitchen counter, John sloshed his friend Jack Daniels into two glasses. What a night. By the time the firefighters reached Wingate Estate and got the fire under control, the main house was destroyed along with any secrets it might hold. He and Andrea had told their story to the police and the fire inspector. It wouldn't take long before Mylinski heard about the fire and their involvement. He just hoped to God that in that time, he and Andrea would find some kind of evidence pointing to Wingate Kirkland's real murderer.

He handed one of the glasses to Andrea. "Drink up. You need it."

Andrea tried to smile, but failed miserably. She'd handled the fire at Wingate Estate as well as she had dealt with the shooting in Chicago. But even though she'd kept her wits together and had led them to safety, he could tell the stress of the last few days was wearing on her.

He threw back the contents of his glass. The whiskey burned down his throat, clearing away the residue of smoke.

Andrea didn't move. She merely stared into her glass, her eyes sunken. Shell-shocked. "I hope Marcella's all right." Ever since they'd escaped from the fire, Andrea had been on the phone trying to reach Marcella Hernandez at her. home. But despite numerous calls, she hadn't had any luck.

"Her car wasn't at the house. For all we know, she decided to drive to the police station instead of calling."

She nodded. "I hope you're right. I just worry. She has no family. Wingate was all she had. That and Wingate Estate." She held her hand over her mouth, as if she suddenly remembered what had become of Wingate Estate. "The fire is going to devastate her."

John's hand moved of its own accord, reaching out and resting on Andrea's arm. She was quite a woman. After all that had happened to her, she was still thinking about others' feelings. Others' needs. "What about you? How do you feel about all this?"

She shook her head. "It was a beautiful house. But I'm not really sorry it's gone. It held a lot of bad memories for me."

"And some things you can't remember."

"Yes." She shook her head. "I wonder..."

"You wonder what?"

"I wonder if my memories are gone for good. Like the house."

She took a sip of whiskey. "Sometimes I don't want to remember. Sometimes I just want the past to disappear so I can start totally new."

John nodded. "Everyone feels that way."

"Even you?"

"Especially me."

"What do you want to forget?" She looked at him expectantly.

He drew in a deep breath, filling his senses with her sweet scent. He knew just what he'd choose to forget. All the times he expected too much. Too much of other people. Too much happiness for himself. If he forgot it all, maybe he could take Andrea into his arms right now.

And maybe he could truly believe it would be forever.

He shook his head and poured another three fingers into his glass. "Not the last few days, that's for sure. I would never want to forget meeting you."

A gentle flush stained her cheeks. Lifting the glass to her lips, she sipped, flinching as she swallowed the rest of the booze.

John downed his own whiskey. Setting the glass down, his gaze landed on his overcoat. At least they'd recovered the tapes before the fire, even though their value remained to be seen. He picked up his coat and dipped a hand into the pocket.

His fingers brushed the edge of a single tape.

"No." He pulled the tape from his pocket and groped for the second one. His pockets were empty. "Damn it."

Andrea's eyes flared with alarm. "The other one is gone?"

A sinking feeling descended into John's gut. "It must have fallen out when I stumbled on the stairs."

"It might have survived the fire." Andrea peered at him, waiting for his answer, waiting for some hope.

Hope he couldn't provide. "With a fire that hot…" He didn't have to say the rest. They both knew the tape had been destroyed.

He picked up the surviving tape. "At least we can see what's on this one."

He led the way into his spartan living room. Andrea perched on the edge of his old brown couch as he crossed to the entertainment center. He plugged his eight-millimeter camcorder into the television, slipped the tape inside and switched on the TV. Snow filled the screen, almost as thick as the white stuff outside. Picking up the remote, he eschewed his recliner, instead sinking into the couch next to Andrea.

What he wouldn't give to circle her shoulders with his arm, to have her lean against him, to lounge on the couch watching a movie like a regular couple. Instead he kept to his side, she to hers, the six inches between them as wide and uncrossable as any gulf. He hit the play button on the remote.

A close-up of flesh appeared on the screen. A woman's curvy legs and backside. She stepped out of the camera's path, the camera adjusting to focus on a bed. Then the woman was in the frame again, climbing onto the bed, her long blond hair swinging over bare shoulders and back. She turned on the bed and faced the camera in all her naked glory.

Andrea drew in a sharp breath. "Tonnie Bartell."

Sure enough. There she was, dressed in a blond wig.

John cringed. Was this some kind of sex tape Kirkland had cooked up with his mistress? Just what Andrea needed to see. Hadn't she been through enough? He glanced in her direction.

She didn't look at him, her gaze riveted to the naked woman displaying her charms on the tape.

Damn him. He should have watched the tape first. He should have seen what was on it before he turned it on in front of Andrea. He reached for the remote.

"Wait." She held up a hand.

He looked back to the tape. On the screen, a shadow played over the bed. Tonnie massaged her bare breasts and beckoned for the shadow to join her. John braced himself for Kirkland to crawl onto the bed.

But it wasn't Kirkland.

Andrea gasped. The man moving across the bed on hands and knees toward Tonnie, naked as the day he was born, was none other than Police Chief Gary Putnam.

Chapter Twelve

Standing near the counter in John's kitchen, Andrea lifted a steaming coffee mug to her lips and took a sip. The aroma and heat suffused her senses. She hoped the caffeine would do its work. It had been a long night—one filled with too much worry and too little sleep.

Tonnie had bedded Gary Putnam and two state senators by the time the tape was over. But Andrea and John didn't need to see more than the first few seconds to know the tape's purpose. Blackmail.

Definitely a motive for murder.

John had tried to get in touch with Detective Mylinski all night to no avail. Finally he'd insisted she sleep in his bed and he on the couch. He needn't have bothered. Even as tired as she was, she hadn't gotten a wink of sleep. Instead, she'd spent the night worrying about Marcella, wondering what was on the tape that was lost in the fire, and thinking about John.

At least this morning she'd been able to put her

worries about Marcella to rest. Although the house-keeper was curt with her over the phone, she was all right. As all right as she could be, that is, after learning she'd lost the house she'd so lovingly cared for for the past fifteen years.

Andrea watched John move around the kitchen, cooking up some breakfast. She couldn't so easily resolve her thoughts about him. Or her feelings.

The metallic clink that vaguely resembled Westminster chimes cut through the morning fog still lingering in her mind.

John glanced at her. "My doorbell. It's seen better days," he explained. "I hope to hell this is Mylinski." He walked to the door and pulled it open.

Andrea wrapped her fingers around the coffee mug and tried not to appear as nervous as she felt. She had to stay calm. She had to focus on the positives. The videotape they recovered proved other people had reason to kill Wingate. If Detective Mylinski was as thorough as John claimed, he'd have to consider the men on the tape had reason to murder Wingate. He'd have to investigate them. And maybe that investigation would clear her name once and for all.

Hand on doorknob, John paused. A muscle worked along his jaw. His shoulders tensed under his white shirt.

A bad feeling inched up Andrea's spine. "Who is it?"

"Putnam." John pulled open the door.

Putnam's square shoulders filled the doorway. Cold sunlight reflected off new snow behind him, making his blond crew cut glow like the sun's aurora.

Sweat broke out on the back of Andrea's neck at the sight of him.

"I heard you had some information about the Kirkland case." His eyes moved past John and raked over Andrea. "I guess I should have known she would be here."

Andrea's skin crawled in response.

John shifted to stand in his way, blocking his view of Andrea. "I left that message for Mylinski."

"Al's busy. Guess you'll have to settle for me."

"Thanks for stopping by, but it wasn't necessary." Although John's words were polite, his tone was firm. "Let Mylinski know I'm looking for him. Where is he anyway?"

"In Chicago following up some leads. But then, you'd know all about those leads, wouldn't you, Cohen?"

"Would I?"

"Hank Sutcliffe? Sunny Vale Apartments? Ring a bell?"

Andrea sucked in a breath. She could only imagine what Hank Sutcliffe had told them. Even though she didn't know the man, the way things were going in the case against her, Sutcliffe would probably tell the detective they'd been intimate for years. It was her own fault. If she hadn't told them about Sutcliffe when they were questioning her, Detective Mylinski wouldn't be in Chicago right now listening to his lies.

"Tell Mylinski to call me ASAP."

"This doesn't have anything to do with Wingate Estate burning down last night, does it? Interesting that the two of you were there when it happened."

Andrea cringed. John had warned her the news of their involvement would find its way to the police. She was hoping it wouldn't happen this fast.

"What were you doing there last night?" Putnam's tone suggested he already had a few ideas of his own on the subject.

John shrugged. "Picking up some clothes for Andrea."

Putnam shifted to the side and peered at Andrea around John's shoulder. "Strange that she's still wearing the same sweater as yesterday. It must be a favorite."

"It is."

"Why were you really there?"

"I'll explain to Mylinski when he gets back."

"You'll explain to me. If it has something to do with the Kirkland case, I need to know."

"I'll wait for Mylinski. Thanks."

Putnam's upper lip curled with disrespect. "What makes you think anyone involved in this investigation would give a damn what you have to say about this case?"

"Back off, Putnam. I have evidence this time."

"Evidence? Don't tell me. You've discovered something that proves Andrea here is innocent of shooting her husband. No, better yet, something that proves someone else did it."

"Something like that."

Putnam threw back his head and let out a guffaw. "Any so-called evidence that you came up with is worthless. You aren't exactly objective. In fact, you aren't on law enforcement's side at all on this case. You might as well be her goddamned defense attorney."

"Tell Mylinski I called, will you?"

Putnam jabbed John's chest with his index finger. "I know all about you. How you messed around with that other case. How you're messing around with this case." He leered at Andrea.

She shivered with disgust. It was all she could do to keep from glancing over her shoulder at the video-tape resting on the living-room entertainment center. How she'd love to grab it and cram it down Putnam's throat.

John reached for the door. "Goodbye, Putnam."

"You're done, Cohen. You're as good as off this case. And if Dex Harrington has any balls, you're out of a job, too."

John shut the door with a thunk, wood cracking against wood. Heaving a deep breath, he turned to look at Andrea.

Andrea gripped her coffee cup until her fingers went numb. "Is what he said true? Will you be fired for helping me?"

His lips thinned into a bloodless line. "I guess we'll find out."

BY THE TIME John reached his office late that morning, he had a message waiting from Dex. A summons for an urgent meeting. Great. Apparently Putnam had done exactly what he'd threatened. No surprise there. If Putnam was the driver of the black truck, he had to be worried about what they might have seen last night at Wingate Estate. What better way to discredit anything John said than to have him thrown off the Kirkland murder case for misconduct?

Or worse?

John thought of the pallor of Andrea's face when she'd turned to him after Putnam's exit. Clearly she hadn't considered the possible ramifications to John's career as a result of helping her. He wished she wouldn't worry about that now. Not when her life was at stake. Her freedom. Compared to that, his career woes were unimportant at best.

He pulled open his office door and stepped into the hall. He might as well get this meeting with Dex over. At least then he'd know where he stood. Once he knew that, he could figure out what he had to do to keep Andrea from going to prison for a crime she didn't commit.

He hadn't quite reached Dex's office when he heard a booming bass voice echo down the hall. His heart stuttered. He'd know that voice anywhere. Over the years he'd grown to associate it with justice.

He gave a quick knock on Dex's open door as he swung around the corner and strode inside.

Judge Gerald Banks stood in the middle of the office shaking hands with Dex.

John tried to ignore the bad taste in his mouth. He used to be reassured that justice would be carried out whenever he saw Judge Banks hobnobbing with the DA. Not anymore. Now it seemed like they were stacking the deck against the accused.

My how things had changed.

"Hello, Cohen," the judge boomed. "I've read in the media that you're working the Kirkland case."

John nodded. The judge hadn't merely read it in the paper, he'd seen John at the house the night Kirkland's body was found. Of course after John's impending meeting with Dex, he probably would no longer be on the case. "Of course if Andrea Kirkland goes to trial and draws your number, I trust you'll be recusing yourself, judge."

The judge raised bushy brows. "Why is that?"

"It won't look good to have you presiding over the trial of your neighbor."

He dismissed John's concern with a wave of his hand. "I've never met Andrea Kirkland. Except for attending a fund-raising golf outing at the course on

Wingate Estate, I barely knew her husband. And no, she wasn't at the outing. So if I'm to preside over her trial, I'll approach it like any other.''

Like any other? That could only mean one thing. He'd give every advantage to the prosecution. With that and the way the evidence was stacking against Andrea, she wouldn't stand a chance.

''It's nice to have you back, Dex. The voters in this county have good taste.'' Grinning, the judge turned to John. ''And Cohen, nice seeing you again.''

As soon as the door closed behind the judge, Dex leveled him with an ice-blue gaze. ''I got a call from the police chief over in Green Valley.''

John sighed. Just as he thought. Putnam must have gotten on the horn to Dex as soon as he stepped out the door. ''Lucky you. I'm sure he had a lot of colorful things to say.''

''He seems to think you're protecting the main suspect in Wingate Kirkland's murder.''

''I'm trying to uncover the truth.''

''That's not how he sees it. I'm ordering an investigation into his charges, Cohen. And while the investigation is underway, I'm suspending you with pay.''

John's gut plummeted.

Dex shook his head. ''I wish I didn't have to do it, but my hands are tied. I can't afford anything that looks inappropriate going on in this office.''

John nodded. He wasn't surprised. Not considering that the DA who occupied the office before Dex had been involved in selling lenient plea bargains to any criminal who could afford his price. After the governor had appointed Dex as interim DA, he had brought the office back to respectability by running a tight ship. John expected he would continue to do so now that he'd been elected to continue the job.

But an investigation wasn't the thing that bothered him. The suspension that went along with it was the problem. An investigation could take weeks. Even if he was cleared of all wrongdoing, Andrea could be charged and half way to trial by the time he was reinstated. "Andrea Kirkland didn't kill her husband, Dex. Putnam is focused on the wrong person."

"And Mylinski? He's on this case, too, isn't he? What does he think about all this?"

"He's in Chicago following a lead."

"So I hear. But that's not what I asked. Does he think you've crossed the line?"

What could he say? "Probably."

Dex nodded. "Take this opportunity to get away, John. Go on a vacation while this investigation is going on. I don't remember you taking a vacation the entire time I've been with this office."

"I can't do that, Dex." He could never leave Andrea. Not while she needed him. Not until this was over. Hell, probably not even then.

"Kit Ashner will take over the case. It'll be in good hands."

John nodded. Kit was a good attorney, if a little ambitious. Ambition that could be realized if she could win a high-profile murder case.

A hanging judge. An ambitious assistant district attorney. Everywhere he turned it seemed the deck was being stacked against Andrea.

"Is there anything more, John?" Dex looked at him, an expectant lift to his brow.

There was a lot more. A hell of a lot more. But he might as well not waste his breath. If there was ever a man who stuck to a decision once it was made, it was Dex Harrington. Arguing with Dex would get him nowhere. "No. I guess not." He turned and walked for the door.

Reaching the hall, he stopped dead in his tracks and turned around. "On second thought, would you give Kit something from me?"

Dex cocked a brow. "What?"

He reached into his coat pocket and pulled out the videotape. Walking back to Dex's desk, he set the tape on the blotter. "Some potentially exculpatory evidence. It might help her see the case in a different light."

As soon as Andrea saw John's face, she knew his meeting with Dex Harrington hadn't gone well. She sprang from her chair, stepped to his side and grasped his arm. "What happened?"

"Nothing I didn't expect."

"He fired you?"

"Nothing quite so dramatic. A suspension. With pay. He suggested I take a vacation."

"Oh, John. I'm so sorry."

He covered her hand with his. "Don't be. It's not your fault. It's mine."

"What did Putnam mean? About the other case?"

John waved his hand in the air, as if trying to erase her memory of Putnam's words. "It's nothing."

She shook her head. It wasn't nothing. Of that she was sure. "Back in Chicago you asked me to trust you. That street goes two ways. What was he talking about, John?"

He exhaled through tight lips and studied her. Finally he nodded. "I was involved in a case a while ago. There was a witness."

"A woman." She'd gleaned that much from what Putnam had said.

"Yes. She had information implicating her brother in the murder of her boyfriend. The trouble was, when she got on the stand, she refused to testify."

"How was that your fault?"

"I prepared her."

"I'm not following you."

"I was young. It was my second major felony. I liked her. I felt sorry for her. And as a result, I wasn't as careful as I should have been. I didn't grill her as hard as I should have before putting her on the stand. I didn't get a written statement ahead of time. And because she refused to tell her story in the witness box, her brother walked.''

''And Putnam thinks that because you like me, because you feel sorry for me, you're going to let me get away with murdering Wingate.''

''I don't feel sorry for you, Andrea.''

A flush crept up her neck.

He trailed his fingers up her arm, spreading the warmth through her body. ''Helping you is the right thing. Dex will see that in time.''

''And if he doesn't?''

''Screw him.''

Guilt settled thick in her chest. Despite his blustering words, she knew the truth. His career as an assistant district attorney could be severely damaged if not totally over. And it was her fault. ''What if we give them the videotape? Then they can see others had reason to kill Wingate.''

''Others like Gary Putnam?''

She nodded.

''I left it for Kit Ashner. She's taking over the case.''

She nodded. ''At least we still have a chance, then. A chance to clear my name. And a chance to rescue your career.''

John raised his hand and cradled her face in his

palm. "Yeah, there's hope. As long as we're still breathing, there's hope."

She leaned her cheek against his palm. How could something that felt so right be so wrong? Wrong for her and now worse for him?

A sharp tap on the door echoed the staccato beat of her pulse. "You home, Ace?"

John sucked in a breath and turned to the sound. He crossed the kitchen to the door and pulled it open.

Detective Mylinski strolled inside. His shrewd blue eyes landed on Andrea. "I'm glad you're here, Andy. I have a few more questions for you." His tone was dark, ominous, the voice of doom.

Dread squeezed her throat like a strong hand.

"Shoot, Mylinski," John ordered.

"I just got back from Chicago." Although his gaze was on John, Andrea couldn't help feeling he was still watching her, still assessing.

"We heard."

"From who? Putnam?"

John nodded.

"Did he tell you why I went down there?"

"I assumed it was to follow up on the leads I gave you."

Andrea turned to look at John. "Leads you gave him? You told him about Sutcliffe?"

"Yes."

She let out a relieved breath. So she hadn't given anything away that she shouldn't. Detective Mylinski hadn't gone to Chicago to prove she was hiding something, but to follow up on what she and John had learned.

Detective Mylinski shook his head. "It was a bit more involved than I'd bargained for."

Andrea's head ached with tension. "What happened? What did you find?"

"It's not what I found. It's what the Chicago cops found."

She stared at him, willing him to continue.

"They found Hank Sutcliffe. Dead."

Shock ripped through her like an electric charge. "He can't be." Tonnie's accusation rose in her mind along with Ruthie claiming she and Sutcliffe hauled a rug out of Wingate Estate. She didn't know Sutcliffe from Adam. And now if he was dead, he couldn't tell anyone that.

"Why can't it be, Andy? Was Sutcliffe a good friend of yours?"

Something in his tone or the narrowing of his eyes made the back of Andrea's neck prickle. "No. Except for him slamming his apartment door in our faces a couple of days ago, I've never seen him in my life."

"Sure about that?"

"What's going on, Al?" John's voice was a low growl.

"The guy offed himself. Ate a handgun."

Andrea gasped. Even though she didn't know

Hank Sutcliffe, the thought of anyone dying in that horrible way jolted her to the core.

"What makes you think he knows Andrea?" John asked.

The detective's eyes seemed to drill into her. "He had a briefcase sitting on the bed with him when he blew his brains out. It was filled with evidence.'"

"What kind of evidence?"

"Photos of our sweet Andy. Copies of e-mailed love letters asking him to help her kill her husband."

Andrea gripped John's hand. Her breath rasped in her lungs. She couldn't get enough oxygen. "It's impossible. I don't know him. I've never even seen him until a couple of days ago. I never sent him any kind of e-mails or photos. And I never asked him to help kill Wingate."

"That's not all. Your husband's cousin says you and Sutcliffe were good friends. A little too good for your husband's comfort."

"My husband's cousin?"

"A good-looking brunette. Lives in Kirkland's apartment in the John Hancock Building."

"Tonnie," Andrea breathed. "She's not his cousin."

The detective looked at her as if she'd lost her mind. "Actually, she is. Second cousin. Or first cousin once removed. However you describe those damn family tree connections."

"Tonnie really is Wingate's cousin?" She shook

her head. She'd assumed they were having an affair, but did she really have any evidence of that? Didn't she just assume Wingate was sleeping with Tonnie because she was young and beautiful? Didn't she just jump to conclusions about Tonnie and Wingate the way others jumped to conclusions about her?

She thought of the videotape of Tonnie. "Wingate must have let Tonnie stay in the apartment in exchange for helping him blackmail his enemies."

John nodded. "Looks that way."

Nausea swirled in Andrea's stomach. Her head throbbed. Blackmail and sex tapes. Love e-mails to a dead man she didn't know. Suicide. Murder.

She wrapped her arms around her middle. She was going to be sick. "I'm sorry. I have to go. I have to—" She ran for the bathroom. She closed the door behind her and hunched over the toilet. Her stomach retched. Her throat burned.

A fist thumped on the bathroom door. "Andrea? Are you all right?" John's alarmed voice filtered through the door.

She wasn't all right. She was so far from being all right, she couldn't find the words. "I—I'm fine."

"I'm coming in." The doorknob rattled. The door opened a crack.

The thought of John seeing her this way, clutching the toilet, so overwhelmed with weakness she couldn't stand up straight, gave her a shiver of panic. But that wasn't the worst of it. The worst was that she wanted him with her. She needed him. And right now she didn't know if she could exist without him.

She swallowed hard and forced her voice to be strong. "No. I'll be all right. I promise. I just need a minute. Please."

"Okay. A minute. Then I'm coming in after you no matter what you say." The door thunked softly closed.

She took a deep breath and tried to quell her panic. She couldn't go on this way. If she needed John this badly after only a few days, how would she feel after a week? A month? She would be as weak as her mother. As needy. As pitiful.

And what would happen to John? She had already gotten him suspended. What next? Would she get him fired? Would she destroy his life just as surely as hers was being destroyed?

She looked at the little window over the toilet. She didn't kill Wingate. But if she stayed, she would destroy John. And no matter how much she wanted him, needed him, she couldn't do that. She wouldn't.

JOHN WALKED back down the hall to Mylinski. Andrea had said she was all right, but he knew better. Her life had been turned upside down yet again. How the hell could she be all right?

Mylinski searched his face, his brows arching toward his non-existent hairline. "What the hell were the two of you talking about a moment ago? Blackmail?''

John turned back to Mylinski, trying to quell the need to race back down the hall, bust into the bathroom and make sure Andrea was all right. ''We found a videotape of Tonnie Bartell in a hidden safe in Kirkland's study. It will shed a new light on all of this.''

''A tape?''

''A pornographic tape.''

His brows arched higher.

John continued. ''It was a set of two. The other was destroyed in the fire at Wingate Estate.''

''And where is the remaining tape?''

''I left it at the office with Dex. Asked him to give it to Kit Ashner.''

Mylinski nodded, but his brows furrowed in a frown. ''So you met with Dex. Any particular reason?''

John's gut ached to high heaven. Mylinski had missed a lot when he'd been on his short trip to Chicago. ''He pulled me from the case. Kit's taking over.''

Mylinski expelled a breath from tight lips. ''Sorry to hear that, but I can't say I'm surprised. Did he suspend you?''

''With pay, pending an investigation.''

''Damn.''

''Gary Putnam is on the tape, Al.''

"Putnam?" The detective's eyes widened. "How bad?"

"Triple-X. He was under Kirkland's thumb. Maybe he wanted to free himself."

"You're saying Putnam could have killed Kirkland?" Mylinski paused as if he was considering the scenario. Finally he grunted. "I'll look into Putnam. If he's dirty, I'll turn the case against him over to the DA. But after what the Chicago cops found, the case against your girl is pretty tight. It looks like Andy killed Kirkland."

John dipped a hand into his pocket and pulled out a roll of antacids. Peeling off a few, he popped them into his mouth and tried to digest what Mylinski was saying. "What about the tapped phone at Wingate Estate? Have you found out anything about that?"

"It was an FBI tap. It seems they were investigating Kirkland."

"For what?"

"Fraud tied to Kirkland Development."

"Might his murder be a result of that?"

"I checked it out. It doesn't look promising."

"But it's possible." He couldn't let go, not if there was even the slightest chance.

"I'm sorry, Ace. I really am. The evidence says Andrea Kirkland is our murderer." Mylinski shook his head. "I could have sworn she was telling the truth when I questioned her the other day. I wanted to believe her. Almost as much as you did."

John was quiet for a long time. Finally he cleared his throat with a growl. "What happens now, Al?"

"I've got an arrest warrant, John. I'm going to have to take her in."

John sucked in a breath. As the evidence piled up against Andrea, he'd feared an arrest was imminent. But the thought of Andrea behind bars still knocked the wind out of him.

Mylinski nodded in the direction of the bathroom. "Are you going to go in there and get her, or should I?"

"Let me." He couldn't explain why it was so important to him to be the one to break the news to Andrea, to hold her in his arms to comfort her, to whisper reassurances in her ear. He didn't want to think about that too hard. He didn't want to think about the way he felt when she smiled at him. The strength he felt when she slipped her hand into his. Or the need that surged inside him when he smelled the scent of her skin.

John turned away from the detective and forced his feet to carry him down the hall to the bathroom door. Bracing himself for what he had to do, he rapped on the wood.

No answer.

Fear hummed in his ears. "Andrea? Are you okay?"

Still no answer.

The hum turned to a roar. He turned the knob.

Locked. He heaved back and surged forward, laying shoulder to wood. The old lock gave. The door flew open.

An empty bathroom met his gaze. And the only sound ringing in his ears was the wind whistling through the open window.

Chapter Thirteen

Mylinski slipped the cellophane wrapper off a piece of lemon candy and popped it into his mouth. Sucking hard, he watched John with his usual shrewd stare. "This is pretty serious, isn't it?"

John stilled. Mylinski had taken the news of Andrea's disappearance much better than he'd expected. Instead of pulling a gun and going after her, he'd merely fixed John with one of his knowing stares— a stare that was making him plenty nervous.

"What are you talking about, Al?"

"You love her, don't you?"

The words rang in John's ears with the finality of a guilty verdict. He opened his mouth to protest, to tell Mylinski he was dead wrong. But for some reason, he couldn't force a sound from his lips.

He couldn't love Andrea, could he? He'd seen too much, been through too much to believe love existed, let alone to come down with the malady himself. "You don't know what you're talking about."

"Don't I?" Mylinski shot him a crooked smile. "Before you met her you were one of the most cynical SOBs I've ever had the pleasure to know. Now suddenly you believe in innocence. You're willing to put your career on the line to fight for her. You've become more idealistic than God, for crying out loud. What do *you* think is responsible for this personality change? Indigestion?"

"Maybe." John reached into his pocket for his roll of antacids. His fingers grasped nothing but a few scraps of foil and a paper label. He'd run out. Just as he'd run out of explanations for the charge Mylinski had leveled against him.

Did he love Andrea?

He'd promised himself he wouldn't expect too much. Not of other people and certainly not of himself. He'd been let down far too many times. Love was expecting way too much. Love was a sure road to disaster.

He shook his head. He didn't know the answer. All he knew was he couldn't abandon Andrea now. "Let me go get her."

Mylinski tilted his head, considering. "I'll give you twenty-four hours. No more."

John started for the door. He had a pretty good idea where she'd gone. Where she would feel safe.

The only place that was hers.

Reaching the kitchen door, he stopped and turned to Mylinski. "Thanks."

The detective nodded and bit down on the candy

in his mouth, shattering it between his teeth. "Don't make me regret this, Ace."

ANDREA STARED out the window at the pine trees surrounding her little cabin. The snow dusting each green bough sparkled in the moonlit night like diamonds. The rough-hewn logs that made up the walls felt sturdy, solid. The little cabin nestled in the northwoods had always been her sanctuary, the only place she could go to escape Wingate's world. But tonight neither the beautiful view nor the solid walls lent any comfort.

She wrapped the quilt tighter around her shoulders. She'd set a fire in the oversized fireplace, but she couldn't get warm.

She might never be warm again.

It had been cowardly to crawl out of John's bathroom window and steal his car, but she hadn't known what else to do. She'd felt cornered. Powerless. Desperate. And she'd panicked.

She didn't want to need him. She didn't want to hurt him. So she'd run away, just as she had when she was a teen. As if that would make her problems go away. As if that could solve anything.

An engine roared from someplace outside the cabin.

Andrea jumped to her feet. Her pulse picked up its pace, thumping in her ears.

She hadn't noticed anyone following her on the small, two-lane country highway leading to the cabin. Not a car, not a black truck. But someone was definitely outside. Someone had found her.

The police?

The black truck?

She glanced around the cabin. If it was the police outside, she'd immediately give herself up. But just in case it wasn't, just in case the black truck's driver had found her, she needed a plan. She needed a weapon.

Copper pans hung over the tiny butcher-block island in the corner kitchen. She stretched up and took a skillet from its hook. The copper weighed heavy in her hand. Heavy enough, she hoped.

The cabin's front door faced north. To reduce the chilling effect of winter winds, no windows had been cut in the logs that made up the north wall. The peephole was the only way to see outside. If only there were windows in the front of the house, then she could see what she was up against. She would know whether the black truck or a squad car was waiting outside. She would know whether to come out swinging or with her hands on her head.

She peered through the peephole. The dark shapes of distant pines met her gaze. A shadow loomed into view, blocking the moonlight.

The latch on the door rattled.

She sprang back. Holding the pan in both hands, she braced herself, waiting for the door to swing open.

Chapter Fourteen

"Andrea? Open the door." John's voice penetrated the thick wood.

Relief flooded her, making her weak. She lowered the pan and let it clatter to the floor. "John?"

"It's me. Open the door."

She drew in a breath of courage. Grasping the wrought-iron latch, she yanked the door open.

And fell into his arms.

His hand came up, smoothing her hair, cradling the back of her head. His other arm wrapped around her and pulled her against him.

His warmth soaked into her. Bolstered her. Filled her. This was what she wanted. What she needed. What she couldn't live without.

No.

Placing her hands against his chest, she pushed out of his embrace. She couldn't lose herself in his arms. No matter how much she craved it.

John searched her eyes. He ran a gentle hand down

her arm. "There's no reason to be scared. It's going to be okay. You're going to be okay."

She shook her head. "I heard what Detective Mylinski said, John. It's not going to be okay. How could it be?"

"Don't worry. We can fight the charges."

"Fight the charges?" His meaning dawned on her. "Detective Mylinski came to your house to arrest me, didn't he?"

"Yes. But we'll fight. You and I. Together."

She stepped back, out of his reach. He didn't understand. She had to make him understand. "No. I can't— You can't—"

"If you're worrying about my career, don't."

His career. Her self respect. She didn't know which to worry about more. "I'm not going to drag you into this, John. I ran away from the police. They're going to come looking for me."

He nodded. "Why did you run, Andrea?"

Her sinuses burned. Tears surged at the back of her eyes. She closed her eyes to keep them from trickling down her cheeks. "I didn't want to need you. To feel like I can't live without you."

The wood floor creaked as John stepped toward her. Although she could feel the energy of him so close, so near, he didn't touch her. He merely waited for her to go on.

She forced breath through a tight throat and compelled her lips to form words. "I need you. So much it scares me. And I was so worried I'd become like my mother—pitiful and weak—''

''There's not one pitiful or weak cell in your body.''

She shook her head. Maybe he couldn't see it, but that didn't mean the weakness wasn't there. Waiting to swamp her, to pull her under.

She squeezed her eyes closed tighter. She couldn't look at him. Not until she told him all of it. Not until she made him understand. ''My mother's need for men eclipsed everything else. Her career, her daughter, even the men themselves weren't important. It was all about her. Her weaknesses. Her needs.''

''You're not like your mother.''

She splayed her hands in front of her. ''I *am* like her. I was so worried about myself, I didn't even consider how you helping me would harm your career. I never thought for a moment about what it would cost you.'' She opened her eyes, looking at him through a veil of unshed tears.

He gave her a sad smile. ''It's not going to cost me anything, Andrea. Nothing important, anyway.''

''How can you say that? You're already suspended because of me. You're already under investigation.''

''True.''

''Wait until they learn you retained a lawyer for me.''

''I can't lie to you. It won't look good. But you're

innocent. I can't let the system railroad you. I can't let you pay for something you didn't do.''

She couldn't stand here, looking at him and listen to him justify what she'd brought on him. She turned away. "I can't let you do this. I can't let you throw your career away on me. Your life—"

"My career is not my life. At least I don't want it to be. Not anymore." He captured her arms and turned her to face him. "When I signed on in the district attorney's office, I did it because I wanted to fight for justice. I wanted to make the world better, safer."

He loosened his grip. Sliding his hands down her arms, he grasped her hands in his. "These last few years I've felt like a factory worker, just one cog in the assembly line, pushing criminals through the system, making deals, going after the win, right or wrong. I lost myself, Andrea. I lost what it was I wanted in the first place. You helped me find it again."

"But—"

"No buts. District attorneys are supposed to advocate on behalf of the people. For right. For justice. You're giving me the chance to do that again."

Frustration burned in her blood and seared her heart with each beat. Powerlessness. "You have to listen to me, John. You can't—"

He pressed his fingertip to her lips, stopping her protest. He smoothed his fingers over her cheek and pushed them into her hair. Cradling her head in his hand, he pulled her toward him.

Her lips parted as if of their own accord. She wanted his kiss, needed it. But she couldn't give in. She couldn't let herself need him. And she couldn't let him sacrifice himself for her. "Why, John? Why do you want to destroy everything you've worked for? Why do you have to be so damn selfless?"

"Selfless? Hardly." A gentle smile curled his lips. "By protecting you, I'm doing exactly what I want, exactly what I need. Hell, I'm being more selfish than I've ever been in my life."

His words raced through her in a rush of heat. Emotion swamped her, pulling her down into the warmth, into the softness. She closed her eyes and let herself fall, let herself drown.

He lowered his mouth to hers. His lips brushed hers. So soft, so gentle, yet underneath she could feel his need. Powerful and barely restrained.

She opened her mouth. His tongue tangled with hers. Danced. Caressed.

His hands brushed over her back. Slipping under her sweater, they skimmed her skin.

A groan lodged in her throat. She wanted to be naked. To feel his skin against hers. To have nothing between them.

Raising her arms, she let him push the sweater over her head. Cool air fanned hot skin. Her fingers found the buttons of his shirt. One by one, she slipped them from their holes. When she reached the bottom of his shirt, she spread the fabric open.

In one movement he shrugged the shirt off his shoulders and down his arms. It fell to the floor along with her sweater.

She moved her hands over the warm, smooth skin of his chest. Her fingertips combed through his chest hair and found the ripples of his stomach muscles. Then she moved them lower. She grasped his belt. Working the leather through the buckle, she unfastened it. Then the button on the top of his slacks. The zipper came next, easing it down to expose his briefs. To expose the bulge of his desire. His pants hit the floor, belt buckle chiming on the wood. She slipped her fingers under the waistband of his briefs. Stretching the elastic, she pushed them down.

She'd never been this aggressive with a man, this forward. But she couldn't stop herself. She didn't want to stop. She wanted to be close, to be warm, to feel everything she'd never let herself feel. To go where she'd never dared. His kiss stoked the fire in her. The touch of his skin drove her mad. She took his length in her hands. She stroked the smooth, hot flesh.

"Whoa." He caught her wrist, stilling her hand's motion. "My turn now or this will be over before it begins."

Moving his hands over her back, his fingers found the clasp of her bra. One move and it was open, sliding over her arms. His hands covered her breasts, kneading, caressing.

Unwilling to wait any longer, she unzipped her jeans and pushed them over her hips and down her legs.

He moved his hands down her sides, over her hips. Grasping her buttocks, he lifted her, fitting her against him. Desire meeting desire.

She wrapped her legs around him.

He carried her to the rug in front of the fire and lowered her onto it.

She clung to him. Need pounded through her. Urgency. As if what was between them was all too tenuous. As if it all might slip away at any moment and leave her with nothing. "I want you inside me," she whispered. "I need you inside me."

His lips moved against hers, then scattered kisses down her neck. Over her breasts. His tongue swirled around a nipple and he took it into his mouth.

Warmth cascaded through her. A moan broke from her throat.

He moved to the other nipple, tasting, teasing, driving her mad with need. She moved against him, stroking him with her body. "Please, John. I need you too much."

He positioned himself over her. With one long, slow movement, he filled her, stretched her.

She opened for him.

He moved inside her, slowly at first, then with more force, more urgency.

She grasped his shoulders, trying to get closer, trying to pull him deeper, trying to make him part of her.

Her muscles tightened. Her entire body spasmed with pleasure. And as she held him close, as she felt the tremor wrack his body, she knew she was lost to him.

He drew back and looked into her eyes. A smile curled his lips and wound its way to her heart. He lowered his head and kissed her. His lips took. Claimed. Promised things she'd never let herself believe possible.

But she believed. With ever fiber in her body, she believed. Because right now in his arms, everything was possible. Everything was right.

ANDREA PULLED her sweater on over her head and took one last look at John. He lay curled on his side, asleep, his arm still stretching out where it had cradled her head after they'd made love. He looked so peaceful, so defenseless. As if he was the one in need of her protection instead of the other way around.

Her chest ached. She could hardly breathe. Making love with him was more wonderful than she'd ever imagined. He was passionate yet tender. Protective yet demanding. And he filled her up and left her aching for more at the same time.

If only the rest of the world would cease to exist and she could stay here curled in his arms forever. Maybe then she'd be satisfied. Maybe then this ache of need that seized her chest whenever she looked at him would go away. Maybe then she could be strong.

But that wasn't to be. The rest of the world wasn't about to go away. And the need in her would never—could never—be filled. Making love with John had made that clear. Because standing here looking at him now, she needed him more than ever.

There was only one thing she could do, only one choice she could make. And it was time she made it.

"I love you, John," she whispered. "More than I can handle. And that's why I've got to do this. For your good. And for mine."

Chapter Fifteen

John walked through the sterile hall of the Public Safety Building—the building that housed the medium-security Dane County jail. His shoes clicked on the freshly waxed floor, echoing the urgent beat of his pulse. He had to talk to Andrea. He had to make her listen. And he didn't have a moment to waste.

He opened one door and stepped into the sally port. Once the first door closed behind him, he waved at the camera looking down at him from the corner. "John Cohen. I'm on my way to the visiting rooms to meet with Andrea Kirkland."

A buzz sounded as the lock released. He grasped the knob of the second door, pulled it open, and entered the hall outside the small visiting rooms.

When he'd awakened to an empty cabin at dawn this morning, he'd known immediately where she'd gone. A call to the jail had confirmed he was right. She'd returned to Madison. She'd driven straight to the jail and turned herself in.

Although the result would have been the same had she stayed with him, he'd wished she'd waited. He wished she hadn't chosen to go through it all alone. He wished she trusted him enough to let him be there for her.

He wanted to be there.

Last night, he hadn't known for certain how important she was to him until the words came out of his mouth. But as soon as he heard them, as soon as he'd seen the tears well in her eyes, as soon as he felt his own heart overflow, he'd known he'd do anything for her.

He had only to convince her to let him.

He opened the door of one of the tiny visiting rooms. Stepping inside, he closed the door behind him and lowered himself into the plastic chair positioned on one side of the Plexiglass.

He'd set up a meeting with her via cell phone on the drive down. He'd asked the sheriff's deputies running the jail to deliver Andrea to the visiting room when he'd arrived. Now he had only to sit back and wait. Wait and worry.

Finally the door on the other side of the Plexiglass opened and a sheriff's deputy ushered Andrea inside the cubicle. She wore a standard-issue prison jumpsuit, the too-long arms cuffed at the wrists to keep from covering her hands. She looked at him with tired eyes. Hopeless eyes.

A pang twisted in his chest.

She sat in the plastic swivel chair. Placing her elbows on the stainless-steel countertop, she picked the closed circuit phone from its cradle and held it to her ear. "Hello, John." Her voice was low, almost husky. But unlike the sexy quality the huskiness had conveyed last night, today it merely served to mask her obvious fear. "You shouldn't have come."

"Like hell. I wish you hadn't felt you had to do this alone."

"It was better this way."

He clutched the phone so hard the plastic creaked. "Damn it, Andrea. I know what you're trying to do. But you don't have to protect me. You're the one who needs protecting."

She pursed her lips. "Maybe I'm doing both, John."

He sucked in a deep breath. She wasn't like her mother. She was strong—stronger than anyone he'd ever known. Why couldn't she see that? "I was hoping last night changed your mind. That you saw how good we were together. That you realized how strong you were in my arms."

"I do feel strong in your arms, John. That's the problem. I have to be strong on my own." She glanced at the cinder-block walls and thick Plexiglass that enclosed them. "Now I have no choice."

He opened his mouth to talk some sense into her, to make her see. He closed it without uttering a word. It wouldn't do any good to go down that path again.

The more he insisted she was strong, the more she would protest. And the last thing he wanted to do now was drive her further away. "At least tell me you called Runyon."

"I let him go."

He let out a groan. "Why? You're facing a murder charge, for God's sake. You need an attorney."

"I don't have the money for his retainer. You heard Joyce. What the police didn't freeze, her lawyers have tied up with a lawsuit."

"I'll give you the damn money."

"Absolutely not. I have to take care of this myself. I'll use the public defender's office."

"You're protecting me again, aren't you?"

Her lips flattened into a line. "I've gotten you in enough trouble."

"If I'm in any trouble, it's because I chose to put myself there."

"To protect me. And I'm not going to let you do it any more. I can take care of this myself, John. I'll be all right. Really."

He wanted to believe her. And if she was talking about swimming free of a submerged car, dodging bullets in the streets of Chicago or escaping a burning house, he might even buy it. But Mylinski had given him a hint of the evidence against her. And even though he only knew the Cliff's Notes version, it was enough to know this wasn't the case for an overworked public defender. And it sure as hell wasn't something she could handle on her own. "If you won't let me pay for Runyon, I'll resign from the DA's office and represent you myself."

Her eyes flew wide. "You can't—"

"I can. And I will."

"No." She leaned forward, gripping the phone so hard her knuckles turned white. "You can't throw your career away. I won't let you."

"Like I told you last night, before you came along, this career didn't mean a damn thing to me. You're the one who gave my career meaning. You're the one who gave my *life* meaning."

She shook her head.

He had to make her understand. He had to make her see the truth. "Without you I wouldn't have a career worth saving."

She shook her head again. "But it *is* worth saving. That's the point. *You're* worth saving. I'm not going to drag both of us down." She returned the phone to its cradle. Swiveling her chair to the side, she stood. The deputy opened the door. She paused, looked over her shoulder and mouthed the words *I'm sorry*.

ANDREA FOLLOWED the deputy back to her cell. When she'd thought of jail, she'd always pictured a small barred cell, concrete floors, a cot and a toilet with no seat. The reality of jail was quite different.

She walked into the room she shared with around twenty women. Bunk beds lined the back wall, a television hung from the ceiling and hard molded plastic seats were anchored to tables which dotted the floor. At the front of the room, a small booth was separated from the rest of the room by thick glass. In this room, a deputy sat, watching the inmates around the clock. It was like living in a crowded fish bowl.

She lowered herself to her assigned seat and wrapped her arms around herself. Seeing John had been even harder than she'd imagined. It seemed cruel not to be able to touch him, to hold him, to wrap her arms around him and press her lips to his.

But it was for the best. She knew that better than she knew her own name. In some part of her mind, she'd thought that by giving in last night, by making love with him, she might sate her need for him. She couldn't have been more wrong. Seeing him today had proved that. She should be grateful for that Plexiglass between them. Touching him could only make matters worse.

For him and for her.

The shuffle of footsteps on the hard floor cut through her thoughts. She looked up at a large woman staring down at her. The other inmate lowered herself into the seat next to Andrea and forced a magazine into her hands. Leaning back, she paged through a magazine of her own.

Andrea looked down at the magazine. "Thanks, but I don't want to read right now."

"Open it."

"I'm sorry, I—"

The woman glanced at the female deputy sitting in the glass booth. Then she scowled down at Andrea. "I said open the damn magazine."

The last thing Andrea wanted to do was make this woman angry. There might be a deputy watching, but there had to be corners of the large room the deputy couldn't quite see. Especially in the dimmed light of night. She lifted the magazine in her hands and flipped open a page. "Now what?"

"Now you listen to me, bitch," the woman ground out through clenched teeth. "I have instructions for you. Instructions you damn well better follow."

Andrea braced herself, ready to back down if she could. She'd heard stories about jail turf wars on television, and she wanted no part of them. "I'm listening."

"Ask to meet with the DA. Say you're willing to take a plea."

"A plea?" She didn't know what she'd expected the woman to say, but this certainly wasn't on the list of possibilities. "What do you know about my case?"

"I ain't answering any questions. You just do what you're told." The woman pushed thick brown hair out of her eyes and glanced at the deputy once again. Apparently satisfied the guard wasn't paying attention, she turned back to her magazine. "This is what you're going to do. Plea to murder. First degree, second degree, whatever the hell they offer, you take it.''

"Who sent you?"

"Someone you don't want to piss off. Just plead guilty to capping your old man and you won't have to worry about who sent me.''

"But I didn't kill him."

"You think I care? You plead guilty or John Cohen is going to meet with an accident.''

Andrea's blood ran cold. "John? What does this have to do with John?''

"Just do as you're told or he's dead. And that's one murder that *will* be your fault.''

THE DOOR to John's office flew open and Kit Ashner bulled her way inside. "Cohen, we're celebrating and you're buying the drinks.''

John looked up from the file he was studying with bleary eyes. The last thing he wanted to do was celebrate. He'd barely gotten two winks of sleep since he'd seen Andrea in jail. When she'd rejected his help.

When she'd rejected *him.*

He wasn't even supposed to be in the office. Dex had made that clear when he'd informed him of the suspension. But he couldn't bear knocking around his house alone one more day. So he'd come to the office despite Dex's orders. Hell, he had nowhere else to go. And the really sad part was that with

Andrea shutting him out of her life, he couldn't see that changing any time in the future. "Why not come right in, Kit? Don't be shy."

Kit ignored the jab and slapped a hand on the file folder in front of him, snapping it closed. "Chantel said you were here. I thought you were supposed to be on vacation."

Vacation. Yeah, right. Dex's way of keeping the rumor of scandal out of the office, at least until he knew if it was warranted or not. He gave his best impression of a nonchalant shrug. "You know me, Kit. It's a working vacation. So what's the cause for celebration? Did you see the tape I left for you?"

"Didn't have time. I'm finishing up a trial. Closing arguments tomorrow."

"Make time, Kit. It's dynamite. And if any of my leads pan out, I'll have more for you."

She waved her hand in the air. "Don't worry, Mylinski came by to get the tape."

"Good." John heaved a relieved breath. Mylinski would follow up as he'd promised. If Putnam was guilty of anything, Mylinski would find it.

"So are you going to help me celebrate?"

He forced his attention back to Kit. Andrea was in jail for a crime she didn't commit, and she refused to let him help. He was reduced to sneaking around in order to investigate what leads he had. Other people followed up on investigations he wanted to handle himself. The hole in John's stomach lining probably rivaled the Grand Canyon by now. And Kit wanted to celebrate. "Why celebrate? What happened?"

"It's Andrea Kirkland. She wants a deal."

"A deal?" John didn't hear her right. He couldn't have heard her right.

"That's right. She wants to plead guilty to murdering her husband."

Guilty? Andrea? Kit's words hit him like a sledge hammer to the temple. She couldn't be guilty. He went out on a limb for her. He believed in her.

Betrayal hummed in his ears. Pain throbbed in his chest.

Kit's voice buzzed in his ears. "I've had some guilty schmucks, but I've never had one ask to plead out this fast. She didn't even wait until the preliminary hearing. Guess we don't have to wonder if she did it or not."

Could he have read Andrea that wrong? Had he expected too much of her?

"Maybe she figures she'll get a break with the judge by saving the taxpayers the cost of a trial." Kit whistled through her teeth and rolled her eyes to the ceiling. "If that's the case, she's got one ignorant attorney. Or at least someone who hasn't been around long."

"Why do you say that?"

"The judge was drawn for her case. Didn't you hear?"

He shook his head. "Who did she draw?" He held his breath and waited for the knockout punch.

"The hanging judge himself. Gerald P. Banks. The woman will be lucky if she ever sees the outside of a prison cell again. Hell, she's lucky Wisconsin doesn't have the death penalty."

JOHN TWISTED the cap off his old friend Jack Daniels and lowered himself into his recliner. The chair that had once molded to his body like a lover felt strange, as if it had been replaced by a new model.

Of course it wasn't the chair. It was him. He'd changed. Andrea had changed him.

He lifted the bottle to his lips. Tilting his head back, he let the booze flare over his tongue, scorch a path down his throat and stoke the pain already burning his gut.

Before he'd met her his life had been empty, meaningless. He'd been going through the motions, playing his part in the system. She'd given him something to believe in, something to fight for. And now?

Now, not only was his life empty, *he* was empty as well. A burned-out shell.

He looked at the full bottle of Jack. If this one didn't do the trick, he'd down another. Whatever it took to forget Andrea. Whatever it took to convince himself never to trust another human being as long as he lived. And if it took two pints to do it, what the hell.

He turned the idea over in his mind and grabbed the bottle. But before he could down a second shot, the bleat of the phone cut through his thoughts.

He grabbed it. "Yeah?"

"Hey, Ace. Got a question for you. It's about the Kirkland case."

John kicked the footrest down and sat up straight in his chair. "Shoot."

"I just got a hold of the fire investigator's preliminary report for the Wingate Estate fire, and there's something that doesn't add up."

"What?"

"A gas can was abandoned in the front yard. The gas can we're assuming the arsonist used to torch the place."

"Yeah? Makes sense. I told you we smelled gasoline right before the place went up."

"That's not the weird part. It's what was next to the can that's strange."

John pushed to his feet. "What?"

"A rosary."

At first John didn't think he heard him right. "A rosary?"

"You know, the kind they use in the Catholic church. Whoever set that fire must have dropped it. It couldn't have come from the house. Neither Kirkland or Andy are Catholic."

"No." John's mind raced. He hadn't held a rosary since he was a child. But he'd seen one recently. Oyster shell beads clutched in work-worn fingers. "Neither Kirkland nor Andrea are Catholic, but I know who is."

JOHN BRACED himself on the dash as Al ignored the phenomenon of centrifugal force and swung his beat-up brown sedan into Marcella Hernandez's driveway without slowing. He hit the brakes just in time to avoid a collision with the garage door.

John shot Mylinski a frown. "No wonder the county won't give you a new car. They've seen how you drive."

Mylinski looked at him with innocently raised brows. "What's that supposed to mean?"

"Never mind. Some things are too obvious to be explained."

Mylinski threw open the door and heaved himself out of his seat. John did the same, and soon they were following the winding walk around the garage to the front door.

Mylinski reached into his coat pocket and pulled out a piece of Jolly Rancher candy. He held it out on his palm. "Want one?"

The way his gut ached, the last thing John needed was candy. But he took it anyway. Maybe it would mask the scent of the shot of booze on his breath.

Mylinski unwrapped a piece and popped it in his

own mouth. The sweet odor of watermelon blended with the scent of wood smoke, melting snow and wet autumn leaves. He stepped up onto the porch and punched the buzzer of Marcella Hernandez's little house and waited for the red door to open.

The drapes cloaking an upstairs window pulled away from one corner then fell back in place. Footsteps rapped down a wood staircase. But the door didn't open.

Instead, the faint sound of an electric garage door opening came from the side of the house.

"She's trying to get away." John spun around and dashed down the sidewalk. Mylinski followed half a step behind. As he rounded the house, the garage door reached its full height. And inside the garage, Marcella Hernandez hefted herself into the black truck.

Chapter Sixteen

The black truck's engine growled to life.

Adrenaline pumped into John's bloodstream. He couldn't let Marcella get away. Not again. He dashed into the garage. Grabbing the truck's door handle, he wrenched the door open. Reaching inside, he closed his hand over the keys dangling from the ignition.

Marcella's eyes went wide. She clawed at his hand.

Blocking her against the seat with his forearm, he killed the ignition, pulled the keys out and slipped them in his pocket. "It's over, Marcella. It's all over."

She shook her head and grabbed the wheel, as if she was planning to drive away with or without the keys. Tendons stood out in her neck. Her eyes flashed wide like a frightened animal's.

Mylinski stepped around John and fixed Marcella with an all-business stare. "Ma'am, please get out of the truck."

She shook her head again.

"We know you were the one trying to kill Andrea." Though his heart was pumping double time, John forced calm into his voice. "We know you set the fire. The only thing we don't know is why. We want to understand why. Explain it to us."

Marcella glanced from John to Mylinski and back again. A sigh shuddering through her, she let go of the wheel and slid from the truck's cab. "She had to pay for what she did."

Mylinski held up a hand. "Before you say any more I want you to know you have the right to remain silent." He continued, reciting her Miranda rights. "Do you understand these rights, Ms. Hernandez?"

She nodded.

"All right. Now you said Andrea Kirkland deserved it. What did she deserve?"

"She killed Mr. Wingate. She deserved to die."

A sinking feeling descended into John's gut. The conviction with which Marcella said the words left no doubt in his mind she believed them. And if she truly believed Andrea killed Kirkland, she couldn't have done it herself.

"So you were the one who ran Andrea's car off the road and into the Green Valley quarry?"

"I heard the missus talking on the phone. She was describing how she did it—how she murdered Mr.

Wingate.'' A sob broke from her lips. "I couldn't let her get away with it.''

John shook his head. So the attempts on Andrea's life all came down to Marcella eavesdropping on Andrea's phone call to the police station and misunderstanding what she heard. The tapped phone, the Green Valley police, and the desire to silence Andrea's emerging memories had nothing to do with it. "And at the hotel. You were the one who tried to run us down.''

Marcella nodded, tears streaming down her cheeks. "She called me to tell me to let in the police. She told me where she was.''

"And the fire at Wingate Estate?'' Mylinski added.

"Wingate Estate belonged to Mr. Wingate. Not her. I couldn't let her get it. It's better it died with him than for the missus to have it. Or Joyce.'' She clenched her fists. Her eyes flashed, fierce with indignation. "They didn't deserve anything he gave them. They didn't love him.''

"Not like you did?'' John guessed.

Her tears flowed harder. "He was everything. He was my life. And she took him away from me.''

John nodded. It all made sense. Her attempts on Andrea's life. Her destroying the estate. But one thing still bothered him. One thing didn't add up. "How did you send the street thugs after us in Chicago? Did you know those kids? Were they friends of yours?''

"Chicago?" She held back a sob. Puzzlement creased her brow.

"You didn't send those kids after us?"

She stared at him as if he were speaking gibberish.

He could press the question, but he knew it wouldn't do any good. Marcella may have been the driver of the black truck, she may have tried to kill Andrea, she may have burned down the estate, but she hadn't killed Wingate Kirkland.

And she wasn't the only one who wanted Andrea dead. Or in prison.

John stood back and closed his eyes as Mylinski fastened handcuffs over Marcella's wrists. So many things had turned out differently than he'd originally thought. So many things that he didn't know what to think anymore.

But despite all the surprises, he knew one thing to be true. Andrea Kirkland was no murderer. And he wouldn't believe she was. Not until his dying day. He'd expected too much of people in the past, but he wasn't expecting too much this time. Not with Andrea. She was everything he knew her to be. Everything and more. It wasn't just his gut that told him that. This time it was his heart.

And his heart would never let him give up on her.

JOHN PUSHED his way through the glass door and into the steamy heat of the Easy Street Café. The usual lunch crowd of cops and assembly aides from the capitol turned to look at him. Probably wondering what this outsider could want. Or what would possess him to risk eating in this dive.

He spotted Kit from across the room. She sat at a scarred table with a blonde. As he approached, the blonde turned her head and greeted him with a smile. "Hi, Cohen."

"Hey, Britt." Britt Alcott was one beautiful woman and a hell of an ADA. She'd even done a stint as the head cheese when Dex had been forced to step down for a short time before the election. And on top of it all, she probably made a great mother. She had three kids now, if he remembered correctly. But as much as he liked Britt's company, he hadn't come to see her.

He focused on Kit Ashner's pixie face.

"Hey John, pull up a cup. Britt says this place has the best coffee around."

"I need to talk to you about the Kirkland case."

Kit grinned. "You mean my first big murder conviction? Sure. I'll talk all day about that one. Easiest case I've ever won." She threw him a wink.

John tried not to cringe at her cheery tone. He glanced at Britt. "I need to talk to Kit alone, if you don't mind."

"Not a problem." Britt pushed back her chair and stood. She held up her coffee mug. "I need another cup of coffee anyway. And a bagel to go. I promised Dillon I'd bring one back for him. He has a jury that should be coming back any time now, and he's afraid to wander too far from his office.''

As soon as Britt stepped to the counter, John zeroed in on Kit. ''When are you meeting with Andrea Kirkland to talk about her plea bargain?''

''Tomorrow morning.''

''I need to be at that meeting.''

She looked at him out of the corner of her eye. ''I don't know, Cohen.''

''You've got to do this for me, Kit.''

''Why?''

''Because she didn't kill her husband.''

''What? Are you nuts?''

''She's innocent, Kit.''

''How do you know that?''

He swore under his breath. What was he supposed to tell her? That he could see it in Andrea's eyes? That he could feel it in his heart? ''I just know.''

She pressed her lips into a line and stared out the steamy window at the bustling street beyond.

''Kit?''

She glanced at him out of the corner of her eye. ''I didn't zone out on you, if that's what you're worried about. I'm just racking my brain trying to figure out what the hell I ever did to deserve this. I finally land a high-profile case, a homicide no less, and you tell me the defendant who is begging to plead guilty is actually innocent.''

"Life's a bitch.''

"And then you die. Tell me about it.''

He leaned forward. "So you'll let me sit in?''

Kit took a sip of coffee. Making a face at her cup, she set it on the table. "This coffee is worse than Mylinski's. I knew I shouldn't have listened to Britt. The woman has cast-iron tastebuds.''

"Kit?''

She rolled her eyes. "You know I'm a sucker for your charm. Meet me in my office at eight. You can explain on the way over to the Public Safety Building. And Cohen?''

"Yeah?''

"This had better be good.''

JOHN SUCKED in a breath as the deputy led Andrea into the small interview room at the jail. She looked pale. Every protective instinct in him clamored to help her, to save her. He couldn't let her accept a plea for a crime she didn't commit. He wouldn't. And that's why he had talked Kit into letting him attend this meeting.

Andrea's gaze landed on him. Her eyes went wide.

Kit stood and held out a hand. "Hello, Andrea. I'm Kit Ashner. I'm the assistant district attorney in charge of your case.''

Watching John from the corner of her eye, Andrea shook Kit's hand and the two women sat.

Kit glanced from John to Andrea. "John asked to sit in on this meeting. He wants to talk to you."

"That's not necessary. I've made up my mind. I know what I'm doing."

"That may be so. But we like to make sure we have things right." Kit shoved to her feet. "I'm going to let the two of you talk. I'll be right outside if you need me." She stepped into the hallway. The deputy standing outside swung the door closed behind her.

John focused on Andrea. She was strong, but jail had already taken its toll. She seemed smaller. More vulnerable. Truly fragile for the first time since he'd known her. His gut twisted into a knot. "Kit said you've asked for a plea bargain. Why, Andrea?"

She pressed her lips into a line and kept her eyes glued to the table in front of her. "I don't want to discuss it."

"I need to know."

She shook her head.

Clearly she wasn't about to open up to him. He took a deep breath. Maybe if she knew all that had happened since she'd turned herself in. Maybe if she knew all he'd learned. "The black truck was Marcella's. She tried to kill you. She burned the house down."

A small line creased between Andrea's eyebrows. "Marcella? Marcella doesn't have a black truck."

"Yes, she does. It was a gift. From Kirkland."

"Marcella." She shook her head as if she couldn't believe it. "But Marcella couldn't have killed Win."

"No. She didn't kill him. And she didn't send those street thugs after us in Chicago. Someone is still out there. Someone who wants to keep you from remembering. Or make you take the fall for Kirkland's death."

Andrea crossed her arms over her chest.

"You're playing right into his or her hands by asking for a plea bargain."

"Why are you doing this?" She didn't move, except for the flinch of a muscle right below one eye.

He reached out and took her hand in his. "You're not still trying to protect my career, are you?"

Her fingers were cold, lifeless, and she refused to meet his eyes. "Let them send me to prison. I just want this to be over."

"There's no way in hell I'm going to let you go to prison for the rest of your life."

She pulled her hands from his. Her eyes pleaded with him.

There had to be more that he wasn't seeing. "It's not just my career you're protecting, is it?"

She looked down at the table.

He was on the right track. He could feel it. "Did someone threaten you, Andrea?"

No. That wasn't it. She'd been threatened before. Hell, she'd almost been killed. A mere threat wouldn't cause her to lie about killing her husband. A mere threat wouldn't force her to throw away the rest of her life. It had to be something else.

Or *someone* else. "Did someone threaten *me?*"

Her eyes focused on his face, the fear in their blue depths as loud and clear as a scream.

Chills spread over him. By pleading guilty, she was giving her life for his. He shot to his feet. "I won't let you do this."

"I'm not going to let them hurt you."

"Hurt me?" He leaned forward and slammed the table with an open palm. "Don't you see? By agreeing to spend the rest of your life in prison, you're hurting me more than anyone else ever could."

She narrowed her eyes, as if she wasn't following.

"I love you, Andrea. I don't want to live without you." As soon as the words left his lips, he knew they were true. He loved her with his whole heart, his whole being. And he would as long as he drew breath. "I can protect myself. Better yet, once we get you out of this place, we'll protect each other."

Her lower lip quaked. She pressed her fingertips to her mouth and shook her head. "I can't take that chance, John. We don't even know who we're fighting." She tore her gaze from his. She lurched from her chair, circled the table and banged on the door with an open palm.

Kit opened the door. Looking from Andrea to John and back again, she stepped inside. "So what's the deal?"

Pulling herself up, Andrea looked Kit straight in the eye. "I murdered my husband, and I'm ready to start serving time."

Chapter Seventeen

"Let's get this under way." Judge Banks's voice boomed through the courtroom.

Andrea flinched at the sound. Cold dread pumped into her bloodstream. She wrapped her arms around herself and hunched low behind the defense table.

The judge's hard gaze swept the room. Silence descended over the courtroom as if everyone was collectively holding their breaths. The judge's gaze landed on Andrea. "Mrs. Kirkland? You want to change your plea?"

Andrea forced herself to rise to her feet. After the threat against John's life, she'd insisted on representing herself despite protests from John, Kit and the public defender's office. The last thing she needed was to have to explain why she wanted to plead guilty to a public defender. She couldn't take the chance that anything would interfere with what she had to do. "I would like to withdraw my plea of not guilty and enter a plea of guilty."

The judge glanced over to the prosecution table. "Ms. Ashner?"

Kit Ashner read the list of charges.

Panic hummed in Andrea's ears, making it hard to hear. She looked around the courtroom. Reporters packed the back of the galley, their cameras whirring from the glassed-in media rooms along the back wall. In the gallery itself, she spotted the judge's daughter, Ruthie Banks, her face tight and eyes narrowed. Next to her sat Joyce and Melvin. Eyes cast downward, Joyce studied a piece of paper, probably the speech she intended to deliver during the sentencing phase of the hearing. Andrea had no doubt her sister-in-law would ask Judge Banks to render the harshest penalty the law would allow.

In the back of the courtroom, Tonnie watched the proceedings through dark glasses. And across the room from her, Gary Putnam watched Tonnie.

Next to Gary Putnam, in the gallery behind the prosecution table, Detective Mylinski leaned back in his chair, his shrewd eyes narrowed on her. She couldn't help but wonder what he was thinking. Not that it mattered. Nothing mattered but getting this over with as soon as possible. Because only when this was over would she be sure John was safe.

Her gaze involuntarily trailed to John sitting next to the balding detective. The ache in her chest stole her breath. She hadn't seen him since the meeting with Kit Ashner, but his words still rang in her ears.

Even now, he leaned forward in his chair, every muscle in his body taut, as if he was planning to stop this miscarriage of justice. As if he'd find a way to save her from prison yet.

She tore her gaze from him. She couldn't look at him. She couldn't think about him. Not about how he'd listened to her. Not about how he'd told her he loved her. And not about how she wished she could let herself love him back.

"Mrs. Kirkland?" The judge's voice cut her to the core.

She looked up.

"Do you understand the charges against you?"

She nodded. Summoning all her courage, she forced her voice to function. "Yes, your honor."

"Do you understand you are pleading guilty to a major felony?"

"Yes, your honor."

"Do you understand by entering this plea you have chosen to forego a trial by a jury of your peers and will be subject to sentencing under the law?"

"Yes, your honor."

"Then please describe your criminal conduct in your own words."

She grasped the edge of the table, doing her best to control the tide of fear lapping at her self control. If she wanted to save John's life, she'd better make this convincing. She raised her eyes to meet the judge's gaze. "I was leaving my husband when he surprised me by coming home early. He refused to let me go, so I shot him. He fell to the floor and his blood soaked into the Persian rug.'' She shuddered at the image in her mind, an image that was all too real, even though the rest of her admission was not.

The judge nodded.

At the prosecution table, John called Kit over and whispered something in her ear.

''Your honor?'' Kit said.

''Yes, Ms. Ashner?''

''The people aren't satisfied.''

A frown curved Judge Banks's lips.

''I'd like to request permission to question the defendant,'' Kit continued.

The judge glanced around the courtroom at the people sitting in the gallery, at the press listening from the back of the room. ''Go ahead, Ms. Ashner. If you're sure it's you who wants to ask the questions and not Mr. Cohen.''

''Thank you, your honor.'' Obviously unfazed by the judge's rebuke, Kit focused on Andrea.

Andrea's mind raced. Never in a million years had she dreamed the prosecutor would ask her questions about Wingate's murder. She'd thought she could just say she did it and move on.

''Mrs. Kirkland, what day did you shoot your husband?''

Andrea swallowed hard. ''It was a Monday. The day before the election.'' She was guessing. The last

John had told her, the coroner hadn't been able to determine the exact day Wingate died. She hoped there hadn't been a breakthrough since then. If there had been, she was sunk.

Kit nodded, apparently accepting her answer. "And how did you dispose of your husband's body?"

Andrea tried to recall every detail she'd heard about Win's murder. Hank Sutcliffe had been there. The judge's daughter, Ruthie, had seen him. "I called Hank Sutcliffe to help me."

"And what did Mr. Sutcliffe help you do?"

Andrea searched her memory, landing on a comment Chief Putnam had made while questioning her. "We rolled Wingate's body in the Persian rug, and Hank carried him into the woods and buried him."

"Where in the woods did Hank Sutcliffe bury the body?"

Andrea tangled her fingers together. Never having seen the spot where the police had found Wingate's body, she didn't know the answer. But maybe she didn't have to know. "I wasn't with Hank when he buried Wingate. I stayed in the house and washed up the blood on the floor."

Kit paused, seeming to have run out of questions for the moment.

John wrote something on a piece of paper and passed it to her. She glanced at the paper, then focused on Andrea. "You testified in your statement that your husband wouldn't let you leave as you'd planned. What did he do when he found out you planned to leave?''

That was easy. Andrea knew exactly what Wingate would have done. ''He got very angry.''

''And you shot him because he was angry? That seems odd. Didn't he often get angry?''

''Yes.''

''Why didn't you shoot him before?''

''He threatened me this time.''

Kit nodded, as if this was what she was after. ''How did he threaten you? What did he say?''

''He said he was going to kill me.''

''Your husband had a lot of firearms in the house, didn't he?''

''Yes. He was an avid hunter.''

''He had firearms and knew how to use them.''

''Yes.''

''So when he threatened to kill you, you had reason to believe he could carry out that threat.''

Andrea didn't have to think to remember Wingate's rages during their marriage. She could only wish her mind had blocked the fear she'd felt during those times. ''I have no doubt that he would have killed me if he was angry enough.''

''And that night he was angry?''

''Yes.''

Kit glanced back at John.

John was smiling.

A shiver of fear shot up Andrea's spine. What had she said?

Kit looked up at the judge. "Your honor, the people cannot accept Mrs. Kirkland's allocution at this time. From her statements today in court, there is reason for us to believe she acted out of self defense. I'd like to request a continuance until we can investigate this new development."

Blood crept up the judge's neck. "Are you telling me you didn't investigate this case before charging Mrs. Kirkland?" His growl shook the courtroom.

Andrea's throat tightened as if being gripped by strong fingers.

Kit stood straight and met the judge's glare. "We investigated, your honor. But—"

"But what? If you truly did investigate the case, why didn't you rule out the possibility of self defense before wasting the court's time?"

"I'm sorry, your honor. We had no reason—"

Judge Banks held up a hand. "I don't want to hear your excuses, Ms. Ashner." He focused on Andrea.

She rolled her hands into fists, digging her fingernails into her palms.

"I'll ask you, Mrs. Kirkland. Did you shoot your husband because you believed he was going to kill you?"

Her head throbbed. She groped for a plausible response. "No."

"Why did you shoot Wingate Kirkland?"

"I shot him because he threatened to write me out of his will."

"And did you marry Wingate Kirkland for his money?"

"Yes, I did." Andrea looked down at the table in front of her. She could feel John's gaze on her, feel his disbelief, maybe even his disillusionment. But she couldn't worry about how he felt. She had more important things to be concerned about. Like saving his life.

The judge looked back up at Kit. "You don't need an investigation. You only have to ask a few pertinent questions. Now shall we get on with this?"

Kit shook her head. "I'm sorry, your honor. The people are still not satisfied with the allocution. May I approach the bench?"

The judge sighed, clearly not happy with the delay. He glanced at the press buzzing in the back of the courtroom. "We'll do better than that. I want to see you in my chambers immediately, Ms. Ashner, Mrs. Kirkland. And why don't you come, too, Mr. Cohen, since you seem to be pulling the strings in this little puppet show." Judge Banks rose, his black robes billowing around him.

The court reporter stood.

The judge raised a hand. "We'll straighten this out off the record."

The court reporter nodded and settled back behind her stenography machine.

Judge Banks stepped off the bench and pushed through a door behind the witness box.

Andrea rose and forced her feet to carry her out the door the judge had taken. She could feel John behind her. By talking Kit into challenging Andrea's story, he thought he was doing what was best for her, what was right. He couldn't be more wrong. The only thing that was best for her was to protect him. The only thing that was right was saving his life. She might be afraid of her need for him. She might not be able to let herself love him because of it. But she could never doubt that if anything happened to him, her life wouldn't be worth living.

Whether she was in prison or not.

Once they reached the judge's office, they settled into chairs facing his wide mahogany desk. The judge sat behind the desk like a robed king on his throne. The bailiff stood off to one side like his armed knight.

The judge surveyed the room through hard eyes. Leaning back in his chair, he folded his hands on his belly. "Do you know why I wanted this meeting off the record, Ms. Ashner?"

"No, your honor. Why?"

"Because I didn't want to read stories in the paper about how I reamed you out and ruined your budding career." His booming voice turned to a growl.

Sweat broke out on Andrea's back, cold and clammy.

The judge continued, his voice crescendoing like approaching thunder. "The district attorney took Cohen off this case because he's involved with the defendant. And now you are acting like his little marionette. Cohen may not care about his career, Ms. Ashner, but I presume you care about yours. Do you?"

"Yes, your honor."

"Well you have a damned stupid way of showing it."

Andrea held her hand to her head. The throbbing turned to a pounding that threatened to drown out even the judge's booming voice.

"Now when we go back into that courtroom, I want you to act like a professional member of this bar. And that means you stick to procedure. You do your job. And that job is to convict Mrs. Kirkland. Got it?"

"Yes, your honor."

Andrea leaned forward. Her head swam with pain. She was going to be sick.

The judge's voice crashed in her ears. "And you, Mr. Cohen, will not return to the courtroom." He glanced up at the bailiff standing behind him. "Bailiff?"

The bailiff stepped next to the judge.

"I want you to escort Mr. Cohen out to the hall."

"You're going to convict an innocent woman,

judge." John's voice was low, but it rang with power, with conviction.

The judge sprang to his feet. "She confessed in open court, Cohen." His shout bounced off paneled walls and buried itself in the center of Andrea's throbbing head.

She pitched forward, her head in her hands.

John sprang from his chair. He encircled her in his arms, keeping her from falling to the floor.

Her mind swirled. If only she'd had his warm arms to catch her that night—the night of Wingate's death. The night all of this started.

The night she'd last heard that same angry, booming voice.

Suddenly she was in Wingate Estate, outside Win's study. That voice boomed through the hall. That angry voice. Then the gunshots. And Wingate falling to the floor. Bleeding. Dying.

Clutching John's arms, she struggled to sit up straight. She wanted to see. To know.

But she already knew.

"You killed Wingate." Her voice was muffled, sounding from far away.

John leaned down, his lips brushed her cheek near her ear. "What did you say?"

"You killed Wingate," she repeated. She forced her spine to straighten. Raising her arm, she pointed her finger and leveled it at the judge. "You killed Wingate, Judge Banks."

The judge's face paled, white against his black robe. "What the hell?"

"I remember." Her strength returned with a rush of adrenaline. "I heard *your* voice. I saw the gun in your hand."

"Don't be ridiculous."

"You shot Wingate that night. You killed him."

"You don't know what you're talking about."

John looked from Andrea to the judge. "Kit," he said, his gaze riveted on the judge. "Get Mylinski in here."

The judge sprang to his feet and pushed the bailiff against the wall to one side of his desk. Suddenly a gun was in the judge's hand. And this time it wasn't a memory. Judge Banks pointed the bailiff's gun at Andrea. "You weren't supposed to remember."

John gripped Andrea's hand. He pulled her behind his body and focused on the judge. "Put the gun down, judge. You don't want to do this."

Andrea struggled to clear her mind, to make the crippling pain go away.

Sweat beaded on the judge's beefy forehead. He shook his head. "Kirkland gave me no choice. He had a tape. A tape that would have ruined my marriage. It would have ruined *me*."

John slowly rose to his feet. "You were on the second tape. You and Tonnie Bartell."

The judge didn't answer, but he didn't have to. "He wouldn't listen to reason. I would have paid anything he wanted. But that wasn't enough for him. He wanted me to fix cases. He wanted me to sell out everything I believed in." He shook his head, his eyes sparkling with tears. "I couldn't do that. The bench, these robes are everything. Justice itself. I couldn't taint that."

"So you killed him," John said.

"I had to."

Andrea raised her hand to her head. It was true. The voice, the gunshots, all her memories were true.

John stepped forward. "And you hired those thugs to kill Andrea and me in Chicago."

Judge Banks shook his head. "I was afraid she would remember. Ruthie happened to tell me in passing that she'd called the police station, that she'd seen it all and her memories were coming back."

"And Sutcliffe?"

"Sutcliffe worked for me. He was supposed to get close to Kirkland. He was supposed to steal the tape. The night Kirkland died, I needed help. I called him."

"He helped you bury the body and then tried to blackmail you himself," John said, putting it all together.

"He threatened to talk unless I agreed to reduce his brother's sentence." Judge Banks swiped at his sweaty forehead. The gun shook in his hand. "He wanted me to corrupt justice. Just like Kirkland."

Andrea struggled to breathe. To think. She had to

do something. But what? The judge would see any move she made.

Behind her, she could hear Kit shuffling toward the door, trying to get help. Out of the corner of her eye, she watched the bailiff move slowly toward the judge. She tried not to look at either of them, tried not to give them away.

John glanced in the bailiff's direction, as if he'd recognized the man's plan, too. He stepped closer to the judge. "How did you know we were in Chicago? How did you know we found Hank Sutcliffe?"

"Ruthie overheard Detective Mylinski talking to you on the phone. She mentioned it to me, and I figured it out from there."

"So you had Sutcliffe killed and used him to frame Andrea."

Tightening his grip on the gun, the judge pointed it at Andrea, then back at John. "I had to do something to keep the police from tracing him back to me. So I hired someone else. Someone good."

The bailiff lunged toward Judge Banks. His hand closed around the barrel of the gun.

The judge bellowed. He wrestled the gun from the bailiff's grasp.

A shot cracked.

The bailiff slumped against the desk, then slid to the floor. A dark patch stained his brown shirt.

Andrea gasped. She scrambled to her knees. She had to reach the bailiff. She had to help him.

The judge straightened, pointing the gun at Andrea and John.

They both froze.

On the other side of the room, Kit clambered to her feet and raced to the bailiff's side. Kneeling down, she ripped open his shirt and held the fabric against his wound.

The gun still in his shaking hand, the judge looked from the bailiff to John and Andrea. "Oh God. I didn't mean to. I didn't—" Tears slid from the corners of his eyes.

"It's over, judge. Give me the gun." John reached a hand toward him.

"Not so fast." He rested his finger on the trigger, the barrel still pointed straight at Andrea. "She's the murderer. She jumped the bailiff. She shot him and then shot the rest of you. They'll believe me. I'm a judge. They'll have to believe me." He lifted the gun and pointed it squarely at John's chest.

John's heart.

"No." Andrea sprang to her feet. She dove at John, trying to grab his arm, trying to pull him out of the way. Her fingers clawed air.

The judge squeezed the trigger.

John kept moving. Lunging over the desk, he grabbed the judge's arm. He pulled and twisted, dragging the judge forward, slamming his arm against the desk's edge.

The gun clattered to the floor.

Andrea scrambled toward it on her hands and knees. Her fingers closed over the hot steel. The sound of John's fist connecting with the judge's jaw echoed through the room.

The door to the office burst open. Bailiffs flooded the room. Shouts jangled the air.

"It's over, Andy. Give me the gun."

She looked down at the weapon in her shaking hands. It was over. She handed the gun to Detective Mylinski. The report of the gun still rang in her ears. The odor of burned gunpowder hung in the air. Two bailiffs took over restraining the judge.

John spun around, his gaze finding hers. He crossed to where she stood and gathered her into his arms.

His embrace was so warm, so strong. "You really are okay."

"Of course I am. As long as I'm in your arms."

"When you charged the judge, I was afraid—" She choked back a flood of tears. She couldn't say the words. She couldn't even *think* of losing John.

"The judge was shaking so badly, he must have missed." He reached out a hand and brushed a rogue tear from her cheek. His lips curled in a wry smile. "Come on. Would I let you get rid of me that easily?"

She thought of how he'd believed in her, how he'd fought for her, how he wouldn't let her push him away. "I guess I even need you to remind me how stubborn you are."

His smile faded. He grasped her shoulders and looked deeply into her eyes. "I need you, Andrea. Every bit as much as you need me."

Love infused her, strengthened her, filled her until she thought her heart would burst. "I've been so afraid. So afraid."

"You don't have to be afraid. It's all over. The judge is going down for murder. I'll get the charges against you dropped."

She struggled to shake her head. He didn't understand. She had to make him understand. "It's not just now. I've been afraid since I met you. Afraid of needing you. Of loving you. Of being weak like my mother."

"Oh, Andrea." He lowered his face to hers. His whisper tickled her ear. "If need and love makes a person weak, I'm the weakest man on the face of the earth. And I wouldn't have it any other way."

She closed her eyes, concentrating on the feel of his hands, the sound of his voice, and the strength pumping in her veins. For the first time in her life, she wouldn't have it any other way either. Because for the first time in her life, she realized that her need for him, her love for him didn't undermine her strength.

It was the source.

"I love you, John. I need you. And I know I always will."

Epilogue

John stopped his car in his driveway. Heart pounding, he jumped out, circled to the passenger door, and pulled it open. He took Andrea's hand and helped her out.

She smiled up at him. "I could get used to treatment like this."

"Happy to provide it." He coaxed a smile to his own lips, trying to distract his thoughts from his jangling nerves. There was nothing he wanted more than to give Andrea the royal treatment she deserved for the rest of her life.

If she would have him.

He slipped a hand into his pocket, touching the velvet of the little jeweler's box, as if he had to remind himself it was there. He'd thought of nothing but marrying Andrea since she'd admitted to loving him in Judge Banks's chambers. And although it might be better to give her a chance to settle her life before he asked her, he couldn't bring himself to wait. He'd almost lost her more times than he cared to remember. And now that she was out of jail and to his surprise was ready, he wasn't going to waste one more day.

He had only to find the right moment to pop the question.

He guided her over the few patches of ice and snow still on his shoveled driveway, careful she wouldn't slip. "I've made a few changes to the house so you'll be comfortable staying here."

"I'm sure it will be fine."

He hoped so. He hoped it was so fine she'd want to stay for a long time.

Like the rest of her life.

He helped her up the stairs to the kitchen door. Holding his breath, he slipped in his key, unlocked the door and pushed it open.

Refinished oak floors and green tile countertops inspired by the decor of her northern cabin greeted them. He focused on her face, waiting for her reaction.

Her smile blossomed into a beaming grin. "You redecorated the kitchen for me?"

The warmth of her smile seeped into his soul. "I had the whole house done. I figured it was about time to let some color into my life." It had cost a pretty penny to get everything done so quickly, but it was worth it to see the look on her face.

"It's beautiful."

His throat tightened. "You're beautiful."

She looked up at him, her clear blue eyes so warm and sparkling they stole his breath.

He should ask her now. Get down on one knee and let 'er rip. His pulse picked up its pace.

He'd always prided himself on his quick tongue and lawyer's grasp of the language. But right now it was all he could do to keep his nerves in check enough to string two words together.

"Aren't you going to show me the rest of the house?"

He forced himself to take a breath. "Sure." He'd show her the rest of the house. Then he'd ask.

After they'd shucked their coats, he offered her his arm. "This way."

He led her through the living room, the second-hand couch and his old recliner replaced by new models to go with the mission-style tables and entertainment center. Her oohs and ahs duly noted, he led her through the bedrooms, the bathrooms and the office, each room inspiring more oohs and ahs. Finally he stopped in the same spot the tour began, his question still not asked. And the words still beyond his reach. "Mylinski stopped by to see me yesterday."

"Mylinski? What did he have to say?"

Remembering Mylinski's contrition, John chuckled. "That he knew you were innocent all along."

"Right."

"Actually he wanted me to give you his apologies."

She pressed her lips into a small smile and nodded. "He was only doing his job. I know that. But it's still nice to hear he's sorry for what he put me through. What else did he say about the case?"

"Putnam has been cleared. Apparently your—" he shook his head. He couldn't bring himself to call Wingate Kirkland her husband. Her marriage wasn't a detail he wanted to remember. Not when he wanted to ask her to take a chance on marriage all over again. "Apparently Kirkland was murdered before he'd had the chance to use the tape against Putnam, and the same goes for the state senators. But there's no telling who was on the other tape along with Judge Banks or what favors they did for Kirkland. We'll never know unless Tonnie chooses to talk. She's been charged with extortion."

Andrea nodded. "It's good to know the mess Wingate made is on its way to being cleaned up, and justice will finally be done."

"And another thing. Mylinski found out why Joyce was lying about what day she returned from Paris."

"Why?"

"She was being questioned by the FBI about Kirkland's business. It seems she was involved in some shady dealings of her own, and she was about to sell her brother down the river in exchange for immunity.''

Andrea shook her head slowly. ''So much for her loyal-sister act.''

''Appearances don't count for much.'' A lesson he'd learned the hard way.

''What about the blonde who was helping Hank Sutcliffe with the rug? The one Ruthie Banks saw?''

''We're still investigating but it looks like Ruthie suspected her father was involved and made up that story to protect him.''

''And implicate me.''

''Yes.''

''I'm just glad it's all over, and we can get on with our lives.'' Andrea looked up at him, a smile blossoming on her lips. ''The future looks bright.''

John's gut hitched. This was the opening he was waiting for. He sucked in a breath. ''I love you.''

''I love you, too.''

''That's all I need to hear.'' He reached into his pocket and pulled out the box. Taking a deep breath, he offered it to her. ''Open it.''

Her fingers shook. Using her thumb, she flipped the lid open. A diamond ring sparkled in the sunlight streaming through the window. The ring he'd so carefully picked out.

He was afraid to speak, afraid to breathe.

''Oh, John. It's beautiful.''

He plucked the ring from the box with awkward

fingers. Taking her hand in his, he lowered himself to one knee. He looked up at her. So strong. So beautiful. His throat closed. He opened his mouth, but no sound came.

Damn. He wanted to do this right. He wanted to give her a moment to remember. He wanted to give her every reason to say yes. But his mind was a blank. He reached for the only words he could find. "It's yours. If you'll take it. If you'll have me."

Tears sparkled in her eyes, putting the diamond's radiance to shame. "As long as we both shall live?"

"Longer."

The tears broke free and trickled down her cheeks. She knelt beside him. Moving close, she fitted her body into his embrace. "I'd love to wear your ring, John. I'd love to be your wife."

Joy spun through his mind and settled in his chest. He pulled her close, his lips finding hers, taking, claiming. He didn't need words. He didn't need thought. He only needed Andrea in his arms.

For all eternity.

Is your man too good to be true?

Hot, gorgeous AND romantic?
If so, he could be a Harlequin® Blaze™ series cover model!

Our grand-prize winners will receive a trip for two to New York City to
shoot the cover of a Blaze novel, and will stay at the luxurious Plaza Hotel.
Plus, they'll receive $500 U.S. spending money!
The runner-up winners will receive $200 U.S.
to spend on a romantic dinner for two.

It's easy to enter!

In 100 words or less, tell us what makes your boyfriend or spouse a true romantic
and the perfect candidate for the cover of a Blaze novel, and include in your submission
two photos of this potential cover model.

All entries must include the written submission of the contest entrant, two photographs of the model
candidate and the Official Entry Form and Publicity Release forms completed in full and signed by
both the model candidate and the contest entrant. Harlequin, along with the experts at
Elite Model Management, will select a winner.

For photo and complete Contest details, please refer to the Official Rules on the next page. All entries
will become the property of Harlequin Enterprises Ltd. and are not returnable.

**Please visit www.blazecovermodel.com to download a copy of the Official Entry Form and
Publicity Release Form or send a request to one of the addresses below.**

Please mail your entry to: **Harlequin Blaze Cover Model Search**

In U.S.A.	In Canada
P.O. Box 9069	P.O. Box 637
Buffalo, NY	Fort Erie, ON
14269-9069	L2A 5X3

No purchase necessary. Contest open to Canadian and U.S. residents who are 18 and over.
Void where prohibited. Contest closes September 30, 2003.

HBCVRMOD

HARLEQUIN BLAZE COVER MODEL SEARCH CONTEST 3569 OFFICIAL RULES
NO PURCHASE NECESSARY TO ENTER

. To enter, submit two (2) 4" x 6" photographs of a boyfriend or spouse (who must be 18 years of age or older) taken o later than three (3) months from the time of entry: a close-up, waist up, shirtless photograph; and a fully clothed, ull-length photograph, then, tell us, in 100 words or fewer, why he should be a Harlequin Blaze cover model and how e is romantic. Your complete "entry" must include: (i) your essay, (ii) the Official Entry Form and Publicity Release 'orm printed below completed and signed by you (as "Entrant"), (iii) the photographs (with your hand-written name, ddress and phone number, and your model's name, address and phone number on the back of each photograph), and v) the Publicity Release Form and Photograph Representation Form printed below completed and signed by your nodel (as "Model"), and should be sent via first-class mail to either: Harlequin Blaze Cover Model Search Contest 569, P.O. Box 9069, Buffalo, NY, 14269-9069, or Harlequin Blaze Cover Model Search Contest 3569, P.O. Box 637, 'ort Erie, Ontario L2A 5X3. All submissions must be in English and be received no later than September 30, 2003. .imit: one entry per person, household or organization. **Purchase or acceptance of a product offer does not improve your hances of winning.** All entry requirements must be strictly adhered to for eligibility and to ensure fairness among entries.

. Ten (10) Finalist submissions (photographs and essays) will be selected by a panel of judges consisting of members f the Harlequin editorial, marketing and public relations staff, as well as a representative from Elite Model Management (Toronto) Inc., based on the following criteria:

.ptness/Appropriateness of submitted photographs for a Harlequin Blaze cover—70%

Originality of Essay—20%

incerity of Essay—10%

n the event of a tie, duplicate finalists will be selected. The photographs submitted by finalists will be posted on the Iarlequin website no later than November 15, 2003 (at www.blazecovermodel.com), and viewers may vote via_pin rder, for their own favorite(s) to assist in the panel of judges' final determination of the Grand Prize and Runner-up winning ntries based on the above judging criteria. All decisions of the judges are final.

. All entries become the property of Harlequin Enterprises Ltd. and none will be returned. Any entry may be used for uture promotional purposes. Elite Model Management (Toronto) Inc. and/or its partners, subsidiaries and affiliates perating as "Elite Model Management" will have access to all entries including all personal information, and may ontact any Entrant and/or Model in its sole discretion for their own business purposes. Harlequin and Elite Model Ianagement (Toronto) Inc. are separate entities with no legal association or partnership whatsoever having no power o bind or obligate the other or create any expressed or implied obligation or responsibility on behalf of the other, such hat Harlequin shall not be responsible in any way for any acts or omissions of Elite Model Management (Toronto) Inc. r its partners, subsidiaries and affiliates in connection with the Contest or otherwise and Elite Model Management shall ot be responsible in any way for any acts or omissions of Harlequin or its partners, subsidiaries and affiliates in onnection with the contest or otherwise.

. All Entrants and Models must be residents of the U.S. or Canada, be 18 years of age or older, and have no prior riminal convictions. The contest is not open to any Model that is a professional model and/or actor in any capacity at he time of the entry. Contest void wherever prohibited by law; all applicable laws and regulations apply. Any litigation vithin the Province of Quebec regarding the conduct or organization of a publicity contest may be submitted to the Régie es alcools, des courses et des jeux for a ruling, and any litigation regarding the awarding of a prize may be submitted o the Régie only for the purpose of helping the parties reach a settlement. Employees and immediate family members f Harlequin Enterprises Ltd., D.L. Blair, Inc., Elite Model Management (Toronto) Inc. and their parents, affiliates, ubsidiaries and all other agencies, entities and persons connected with the use, marketing or conduct of this Contest are ot eligible to enter. Acceptance of any prize offered constitutes permission to use Entrants' and Models' names, essay ubmissions, photographs or other likenesses for the purposes of advertising, trade, publication and promotion on behalf f Harlequin Enterprises Ltd., its parent, affiliates, subsidiaries, assigns and other authorized entities involved in the udging and promotion of the contest without further compensation to any Entrant or Model, unless prohibited by law.

. Finalists will be determined no later than October 30, 2003. Prize Winners will be determined no later than January 1, 2004. Grand Prize Winners (consisting of winning Entrant and Model) will be required to sign and return Affidavit f Eligibility/Release of Liability and Model Release forms within thirty (30) days of notification. Non-compliance vith this requirement and within the specified time period will result in disqualification and an alternate will be elected. Any prize notification returned as undeliverable will result in the awarding of the prize to an alternate set of vinners. All travelers (or parent/legal guardian of a minor) must execute the Affidavit of Eligibility/Release of Liability rior to ticketing and must possess required travel documents (e.g. valid photo ID) where applicable. Travel dates pecified by Sponsor but no later than May 30, 2004.

. Prizes: One (1) Grand Prize—the opportunity for the Model to appear on the cover of a paperback book from the Iarlequin Blaze series, and a 3 day/2 night trip for two (Entrant and Model) to New York, NY for the photo shoot of Model which includes round-trip coach air transportation from the commercial airport nearest the winning Entrant's ome to New York, NY, (or, in lieu of air transportation, $100 cash payable to Entrant and Model, if the winning Entrant's ome is within 250 miles of New York, NY), hotel accommodations (double occupancy) at the Plaza Hotel and $500 ash spending money payable to Entrant and Model, (approximate prize value: $8,000), and one (1) Runner-up Prize of 200 cash payable to Entrant and Model for a romantic dinner for two (approximate prize value: $200). Prizes are valued n U.S. currency. Prizes consist of only those items listed as part of the prize. No substitution of prize(s) permitted by vinners. All prizes are awarded jointly to the Entrant and Model of the winning entries, and are not severable - prizes nd obligations may not be assigned or transferred. Any change to the Entrant and/or Model of the winning entries will esult in disqualification and an alternate will be selected. Taxes on prize are the sole responsibility of winners. Any and ll expenses and/or items not specifically described as part of the prize are the sole responsibility of winners. Harlequin Enterprises Ltd. and D.L. Blair, Inc., their parents, affiliates, subsidiaries are not responsible for errors in printing of ontest entries and/or game pieces. No responsibility is assumed for lost, stolen, late, illegible, incomplete, inaccurate, on-delivered, postage due or misdirected mail or entries. In the event of printing or other errors which may result in nintended prize values or duplication of prizes, all affected game pieces or entries shall be null and void.

. Winners will be notified by mail. For winners' list (available after March 31, 2004), send a self-addressed, stamped nvelope to: Harlequin Blaze Cover Model Search Contest 3569 Winners, P.O. Box 4200, Blair, NE 68009-4200, or efer to the Harlequin website (at www.blazecovermodel.com).

Contest sponsored by Harlequin Enterprises Ltd., P.O. Box 9042, Buffalo, NY 14269-9042.

HBCVRMODEL2

HARLEQUIN®
INTRIGUE®

presents another outstanding installment
in our bestselling series

COLORADO
CONFIDENTIAL

**By day these agents are cowboys; by night they are
specialized government operatives. Men bound by love,
loyalty and the law—they've vowed to keep their
missions and identities confidential...**

August 2003
ROCKY MOUNTAIN MAVERICK
BY GAYLE WILSON

September 2003
SPECIAL AGENT NANNY
BY LINDA O. JOHNSTON

In **October**, look for an exciting short-story collection
featuring *USA TODAY* bestselling author
JASMINE CRESSWELL

November 2003
COVERT COWBOY
BY HARPER ALLEN

December 2003
A WARRIOR'S MISSION
BY RITA HERRON

PLUS
FIND OUT HOW IT ALL BEGAN
**with three tie-in books from Harlequin Historicals,
starting January 2004**

Available at your favorite retail outlet.

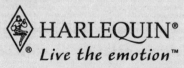

HARLEQUIN®
Live the emotion™

Visit us at www.eHarlequin.com

HICCAST

eHARLEQUIN.com

For **FREE online reading,** visit
www.eHarlequin.com now and enjoy:

Online Reads
Read **Daily** and **Weekly** chapters from
our Internet-exclusive stories by your
favorite authors.

Red-Hot Reads
Turn up the heat with one of our more
sensual online stories!

Interactive Novels
Cast your vote to help decide how these
stories unfold…then stay tuned!

Quick Reads
For shorter romantic reads, try our
collection of Poems, Toasts, & More!

Online Read Library
Miss one of our online reads?
Come here to catch up!

Reading Groups
Discuss, share and rave with other
community members!

For great reading online,
visit www.eHarlequin.com today!

INTONL

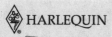

HARLEQUIN
INTRIGUE®
COMING NEXT MONTH

#725 SPECIAL AGENT NANNY by Linda O. Johnston
Colorado Confidential

After someone set fire to the records office at Gilpin Hospital, Colorado Confidential agent and arson investigator Shawn Jameson agreed to work undercover as a nanny to find the culprit. But when he met key suspect Dr. Kelley Stanton and started caring for her three-year-old daughter, he knew he couldn't be the one to blame. Could he protect her from the real arsonist, and win her heart?

#726 OPERATION BASSINET by Joyce Sullivan
The Collingwood Heirs

Detective Mitch Halloran had some bad news to break to stay-at-home mom Stef Shelton—the child she'd been raising wasn't really hers! The two embarked on a mission to find the kidnapper and get her baby back. But as they delved deeper into the mystery, they couldn't deny the growing passion between them....

#727 CONFISCATED CONCEPTION by Delores Fossen

Accountant Rachel Dillard thought she was safe in protective custody. Safe from her boss, whom she was going to testify against, and safe from her mixed emotions for soon-to-be ex-husband, Jared Dillard. But when Jared told her that one of their frozen embryos had been secretly implanted in a surrogate mother, she knew they had to team up to find their child. But would working together tear them apart for good? Or bring them closer than ever....

#728 COWBOY P.I. by Jean Barrett

The last thing private investigator Roark Hawke wanted to do was protect Samantha Howard. The headstrong beauty didn't even want his help—or the ranch she was about to inherit. Then an intentional rockslide nearly killed them, and Samantha was forced to put her life in Roark's capable hands. Could he discover who was trying to kill the woman he'd fallen for—before it was too late?

Visit us at www.eHarlequin.com

HICNM0803